ADVENTURES WITH THE BUTTONWOODS

ADVENTURE.

By Edna Beiler

VITH THE BUTTONWOODS

LLUSTRATED BY F. A. SONDERN

IERALD PRESS, SCOTTDALE, PENNSYLVANIA

TO MABEL
WHOSE INTEREST IN THE BUTTONWOODS
NEARLY EQUALED MY OWN.

Contents

Chapter 1

The Buttonwood Kitchen

Betsy stood in the kitchen door watching Dad Buttonwood drive down the lane. She waited until the old Ford was just a distant dot, then turned with a shiver and went inside.

The big Buttonwood kitchen seemed twice as big as usual that afternoon because it was empty. This was so strange that Betsy almost felt as if she had strayed into the wrong house by mistake.

But no—the funiture was still the same. There was the big wood range, with a stack of diapers warming on the oven door—the long, oilcloth-covered table—the old clock, that had once belonged to Great-granddad Buttonwood, ticking away on its shelf with a row of oil lamps beside it.

1

Betsy sagged down on Mom's old rocker. It was the same place, but it just didn't seem the same without the usual crowd of Buttonwoods, that was all!

By closing her eyes, Betsy could see them all. Dad Buttonwood, with eyes that had crinkles at the corners from laughing so much. Who could believe that hands as big and brown as his could be so gentle, too?

And Mom. They couldn't possibly do without Mom, of course. Nobody else could be so helpful when you were sick or so completely comforting when things went wrong. She always had some little saying to fit the occasion, too. Like, "If at first you don't succeed, try, try again." Or, "Early to bed and early to rise makes a man healthy, wealthy, and wise."

Of course, Mom could be pretty sharp when you were naughty, but even that gave you a safe kind of feeling when she was around.

Then there were the Buttonwood twins, who weren't really twins at all. The rest called them that, partly because they had the same birthday (although Crish was seven and Peter eight) and partly because they stuck together like cockleburs. Crish didn't always appreciate the queer kinds of pets that Peter lugged around (fishworms or beetles or little turtles), but she put up with them anyway.

The older children all felt responsible for "the little ones," as they sometimes called the twins (to their disgust). But Betsy felt the most responsible of all, because she was twelve and the oldest. Sometimes, when the twins were everlastingly underfoot, or a bird's nest (from Pudge's collection) tumbled on her head from a closet, or perhaps when somebody interrupted her for the tenth time before she finished the chapter in her book—well, Betsy had felt that it might be rather nice to be an only child. But during the week of Small Susie's birth, while the others were away, she changed her mind!

Pudge came next to Betsy in age and Flora was two years younger. There were lots of times when they all crowded into the kitchen, just settling down wherever there was room (on the long bench behind the table, or on the wood box, or perhaps even on the faded rag rug in front of the range), and had good times together. No wonder the kitchen seemed empty and quiet now!

"It really does seem funny without them," Betsy said out loud to herself.

"What did you say?" Mom called from the dining room.

Betsy went in to her. Mom was settled on the sofa, with two pillows behind her back and the baby's crib beside her.

"I was just thinking how queer it seems without the others," Betsy explained. "It doesn't seem like our house at all. Did you notice, Mom?"

"Indeed I did!" Mom said heartily. "I haven't felt at home all week, it's been so quiet."

"Cousin Carolyn was nice, but I'm rather glad she's gone," Betsy said.

Mom smiled at her. "I know just how you feel. She's a good girl and I appreciated her help—but I'm glad that it will be just us again."

"Yes, but all of us!" Betsy added.

Suddenly, the baby made a little mewing sound, almost like a kitten. Betsy bent over her.

"What's the matter, Susie dear?" she asked.

Small Susie sucked in her lower lip, then blew it out again.

"She's getting hungry, I guess," Mom said. "You'd better warm her bottle right away."

"I'll say!" Betsy agreed. "I never heard anybody make as much noise for her size as she does when she's hungry."

A few minutes later she was back with the bottle.

"Here you are, Miss Muffet," she said.

She picked up Susie and cradled her against her shoulder. She and Mom smiled at each other.

"Isn't she warm and little and dear, Mom?" Betsy said.

Mom nodded her head. "You children were all cute when you were tiny tots, Betsy. I remember you had a wisp of a curl right on top of your head and eyes that were as bright and brown as a little sparrow's."

"Didn't the twins squeal when they were here to see her, though?" Betsy said.

Then she wished she hadn't mentioned it. The twins were having a hard time at Granddad's that week, and she was sorry she had reminded Mom of it.

Mom sighed. "Yes, it will be nice to have all the Buttonwoods back here where they belong," she said.

A few minutes later they heard a car door slam. In a minute the twins and Flora dashed in, while Dad and Pudge followed with the suitcases.

"Hey—it's nice to be back," Peter said.

"Where's the baby?" Flora demanded.

When Crish saw what Betsy was doing, she gave a howl. "That's not fair, Betsy Buttonwood! You've been home helping take care of her every single day since she came, while we got sent off to Granddad's. It's my turn—"

"Well, Granddad's was better than Uncle Daniel's, any day," Flora said. "Mom—you should see their kitchen."

"I have seen it," Mom reminded her. "It's much prettier than ours."

"Prettier! Who cares about pretty? It's so clean that you wouldn't dare dribble a cracker crumb anywhere. And it's always chilly around the edges, too."

Flora leaned over the edge of the sofa. She put her face close to Mom's. "Besides, it just doesn't feel nice and friendly, like ours," she said.

"I didn't like it at Granddad's, either," Peter complained, edging around to get next to Mom. "Oh, it's fun to go for a weekend but not to stay all the time! Their house was so still that when you made a noise, it echoed. Honest, Mom. And I was real lonesome for our own house."

By then Crish was settled in a chair, giving Susie her bottle. She looked up at Peter.

"Not after you caught Midget Mouse, you weren't," she said. "Before that, you did seem kind of dull."

"Peter!" Mom and Dad said together.

Peter looked down at his feet without saying so much as a word.

"It was so still over there, I just couldn't stand it," he said finally in a whisper. "After school—well, I just hated to go indoors; so I played in the woodshed. And this little wood mouse came creeping out one day."

He looked around and the interest in every face seemed to give him confidence. "He was just as cute as he could be, with his white breast and neat little paws," he insisted. "And I was lying real still when he crept up close—"

Mom and Betsy looked at each other. They knew that Peter had been crying because he was homesick, but, of course, he wouldn't want to admit that.

"Anyway, I just made a quick grab—and there he was!" With that, Peter put his hand into his pocket, then held it out. In it was Midget Mouse.

"Can I keep him, Mom? Please? Please, can I?"

"*May* I, you mean," Mom corrected automatically. She looked at Dad. "I hardly know—"

Betsy knew what she was thinking. They didn't really want a mouse around, but Mom hated to say *no* to Peter just then.

Then Dad gave a kind of half-nod. Mom smiled, and Betsy knew that Peter had won.

"Just remember—a mouse in the hand is worth two in the wood box," Mom warned.

They all laughed, because they knew that Mom had adapted one of her little sayings for Peter's benefit.

"If I hurry up and get supper on the table, Dad and Pudge can eat before they do the chores," Betsy said briskly.

She bustled out to the kitchen and it certainly didn't seem empty or strange now. Flora came trailing out a minute later, with the baby in her arms, while Crish carried the empty bottle. Then Dad helped Mom walk out to her rocker—and after that, everybody else was right there, too.

The baby whimpered for a bit, then nodded her head sleepily.

"Let me put her to bed," Dad said. Betsy noticed again how gentle his big brown hands were as he lifted Small Susie to his shoulder.

Just then Crish came to lean on Mom's knee. "I do think our kitchen is the nicest place in the whole world," she said.

"Oh, no, it isn't!" Betsy said quickly. She smiled at Mom over Crish's head.

Crish looked indignant, but before she could speak up, Betsy went on. "It needs some Buttonwoods in it before it's really nice," she said. "A lot of Buttonwoods, in fact."

"All eight of us together," Mom added softly.

Chapter 2

Here Comes Hooty!

Pudge, Betsy, and Flora Buttonwood, just home from school, burst into the big kitchen, arguing at the top of their voices.

"I don't care what you say, Pudge Buttonwood!" Betsy thumped her books on the table. "Miss Temple is so fair, and that Windy Winfield has no business talking like that."

"I'll say!" Flora added, as she clattered her lunch box into the sink. "He makes me sick with his biggety talk, anyway!"

"Oh, girls," Pudge groaned in disgust. "They never give up. I just proved to you that Win's right, but you still keep insisting—"

"Pudge! Girls!" Mom put her hands to her ears. "What is this?"

8

They all tried to tell her at the same time, but she stopped them. "Don't all talk at once now. Betsy, you go ahead. The rest can have a turn later."

"Well, look, Mom—you remember that new boy at school? His family moved in behind Satterlie's store, where Bakers used to live. And he's been stuffing Pudge with all kinds of fibs about Miss Temple."

"They are not fibs—" Pudge began, but Mom stopped him.

"No, Pudge." Her voice was firm. "Let Betsy finish first."

Betsy took a deep breath. "Windy says that Miss Temple isn't fair. And he claims she has pets and that she's always picking on him. And—well, we were just telling Pudge."

"So I heard," Mom said dryly. "Just remember—'It isn't always the donkey that brays the loudest that makes the most sense.'"

The three young Buttonwoods looked at each other. Mom was always coming up with little sayings like that, but this was a new one to them. They wondered whether she might have made it up, just for their benefit!

"Now, Pudge, it's your turn," Mom said.

"Flo and Betsy just talk like that because they don't like Windy—that's all," Pudge said. "Miss Temple really does pick on him. I've noticed it myself. The minute anything goes wrong, she's down on him right away."

"You used to like Miss Temple, Pudge," Flora said. "It's just since Windy came—"

"No fair—I haven't finished!" Pudge told her. "Windy just pointed out some things I hadn't noticed before. Miss Temple isn't so hot as a teacher. You girls just don't know any better. You'd like her no matter what she did."

"Really, I don't know what's come over you children," Mom said. "The way you talk to each other!"

"Well, I never knew girls could be so stupid—" Pudge began.

"That's enough, Pudge—all of you!" Mom's voice had an edge to it that they seldom heard. "I will not have you talking to each other like that. Betsy and Flo, go and change your clothes. And not another word about this out of either one of you—now mind!"

As soon as the girls had gone, she went on. "Now, Pudge, let's talk this over for a bit. Isn't it true that you are different since Windy Winfield came?"

She paused a moment, and the quiet in the big kitchen seemed strange after so much noise. Pudge could hear little sounds (the tick-tock-a-tock of the big clock and the humming sound the teakettle made from its spot halfway back on the range).

"But Miss Temple does pick on Windy, Mom," Pudge said. "The minute anything happens, she jumps him about it."

"I wonder—isn't that because, in one way or another, Windy is usually at the bottom of any kind of mischief?"

The way Mom always knew things like that baffled Pudge!

Why, you'd think she had been right in the little one-room schoolhouse herself.

"I'd be careful about letting myself be influenced too much," Mom went on. " 'Birds of a feather flock together,' remember? You can be friendly, of course. But if you chum with someone like this, you're bound to catch some of his attitudes."

Pudge looked at Mom. "But I haven't, Mom. Really I haven't."

"Really! Just think a minute, Pudge. How about that way you have of saying 'Oh girls'? Didn't that come from him? And this talk about Miss Temple certainly never showed up until after he came. I'd be careful about following Windy's lead too much."

"Okay," Pudge agreed, but he knew it would be hard. There was something about Windy—the funny things he said, the bold kind of mischief he pulled off, the jokes he played— that Pudge couldn't help liking.

Mom's voice pulled Pudge away from his thoughts again. "You'd better run and change, too. Do your chores right away. Dad said to tell you that you'll have to carry oats from the barn for the chickens—he won't be back with the feed in time for tonight."

Pudge hustled out of his school clothes as fast as he could. He'd do the chickens first and then begin on the barn chores. Maybe he could get most of them done by the time Dad got

2

home. It was fun to surprise him like that—the look on his face always made Pudge feel warm and happy inside.

Once outside, Pudge was in such a hurry that he cut through Little Orchard instead of going around by the lane. But he stopped fast enough when a sudden commotion started right above his head—blue jays shrieking angrily. Peering upward, he noticed an owl sitting on a limb, while the jays circled around to tease and taunt. Pudge had read in a book about what happened to any owl that dared stray out before dark, but he'd never seen anything like it before.

Just then, an unusually bold blue jay flew right at Mr. Owl and made him lose his balance. As he dropped downward, Pudge grabbed him.

"Now, I've got to get busy, but I'll take a good look at you later," he said, tucking him under his jacket.

Mr. Owl spent an hour under an overturned basket before Pudge finished his chores and took him into the kitchen. The other children all crowded around and clamored to hold him (except Small Susie, of course). Even Mom stopped long enough to take a good look.

"Maybe Peter could have him for a pet, too," Flora suggested with a giggle.

"I'm afraid he wouldn't get along very well with Midget Mouse," Pudge said with a grin. "Better keep Midget out of the way, Pete, because this fellow would really enjoy him for supper."

Peter put his hand into his pocket to make sure that Midget was safe. "Don't worry—I will," he promised.

After a bit, Dad came stamping in. "We must have a brownie on the place," he said with a grin. "A brownie who enjoys doing the chores. Although my guess is that it's a brownie with brown hair and freckles. Thanks a lot, Pudge. Hey—what do we have here?"

"A barn owl. See his heart-shaped face? 'Sfunny how anybody as fast and alert as this fellow is at night can be so slow and stupid during the day!"

"I know!" Betsy said suddenly. "Let's take him to school! We were studying about helpful birds and animals last week, remember? He'd fit in just fine, wouldn't he, Pudge?"

Pudge looked at Mom. "Yes, I think he would," she said. "After the children have seen him, I'd suggest that you let him go again. We have enough pets already—and I don't think he would get along too well with Midget, anyway."

"He should have a name," Flora said. She looked at his solemn face and blinking eyes. "Hoo-hoo are you?"

"Hooty! That's a good name for him," Pudge said.

Hooty slept in the granary that night and went to school under Pudge's coat the next day. The other children were all interested, except Windy Winfield.

"Aw—just an old owl! Why all the fuss?" he said. "Of course, you could have some fun with him if you worked it right." He winked at the other fellows and they all grinned.

"Better watch him, Pudge," Flora whispered. "He'll be up to something first thing you know."

Pudge really meant to keep an eye on Windy. Then Miss Temple drove up. The other children all crowded around to get a better look, too. But when Miss Temple told him that she'd like to have a report about owls for the whole school, it drove every other thought out of Pudge's mind completely. She told him to find out as much as he could from the library books, and after recess, he could tell the others.

Pudge didn't like making speeches, because he always felt so hot and bothered. But this was different. He could talk about something he was really interested in; so he tucked Hooty under a box in the cloakroom and went to his seat with a light heart.

At recess time Windy yelled, "Now, let's not spend our whole time mooning over a stupid owl. Who wants to play andy-over?"

Everybody did, of course; so they all trooped out. By the time recess was over, the box in the cloakroom was tipped over and Hooty had disappeared.

"I guess it wasn't weighted down enough," Miss Temple said. "That's too bad, but you can still tell us about owls, Pudge."

"Okay," Pudge said, but he had an uneasy feeling inside, and the smug look on Windy's face didn't help it any, either.

In his talk, Pudge told the whole school all he knew about

owls. He described their wonderful eyes and sharp ears, that could see and hear things far below in the grass.

"They even have a little extra eyelid, so thin they can see right through it. They use that to protect their eyes while they fly," Pudge explained.

"Aw, I don't believe it. He's making that up, Miss Temple," Windy said suddenly.

That was just the kind of smart remark that he sometimes made in class, too. Miss Temple frowned the children into silence, but Pudge felt guilty as he went on. He had giggled at Windy's jokes himself, more than once.

"The shoe's on the other foot now." Pudge could almost hear Mom saying that!

"That was excellent, Pudge," Miss Temple said when he finished. "And now we must get back to work again. Second grade, come forward for reading, please."

After that, things happened so fast that Pudge couldn't keep up with them. He was getting out his geography book; so he didn't see Miss Temple walk over to her desk. But he did hear her gasp, in a strangled kind of way. And he saw plainly enough that she pulled Hooty out of the drawer she had just opened.

"I wonder who might have considered this a joke?"

Her voice had an icy edge to it that sent a shiver down Pudge's spine. He glanced across at Windy and was glad he wasn't in his shoes.

"We all know who brought Hooty to school," Windy said without winking.

Pudge's mouth fell open. He pulled in his breath, real hard because he was so surprised. And angry, too. But Miss Temple didn't give him a chance to defend himself.

"Put him in the cloakroom until time to go home, Pudge," was all she said.

The rest of the day was two days long for Pudge. He couldn't seem to keep his mind on his lessons, and so he was mighty glad when it was time to go home.

"Wait, Pudge," Flora said, as he grabbed Hooty to go.

"What do you want?" Pudge growled.

"I have something to tell Miss Temple. You come on in so you'll hear it, too."

She sounded so mysterious that Pudge got interested in spite of himself. He stepped back into the schoolroom, with Hooty tucked under his arm.

Flora went up to Miss Temple. "I know who put Hooty in your desk today," she said.

Miss Temple straightened up. So did Pudge.

"You must not make a guess about something like that, Flora. You have to be absolutely sure," Miss Temple said gravely.

"I am sure. I happened to see Windy sneak off during recess; so I followed along and peeked in at the window. It was that time when you were outside settling a fuss between

Ray and Nick, remember? I saw Windy put Hooty into your desk."

"Why didn't you tell me, Flora?" Miss Temple asked.

"I—I hated to tattle," Flora said. "And I wouldn't have told now if he hadn't blamed it on Pudge. I knew Pudge wouldn't do a thing like that and I didn't want you to think so, either."

"But I didn't think so—not for a minute."

Pudge and Flora stared at Miss Temple. "But you didn't say anything—" Pudge protested.

"What could I say?" Miss Temple's eyes twinkled. "Next thing I would have been picking on poor Windy again."

Flora laughed, too. And in a minute Pudge joined in. It did him good, and he knew that in the days ahead he would be on Miss Temple's side for sure.

That evening Betsy and Flora and the twins trailed after Pudge, down to the sugar grove below the barnyard. He was carrying Hooty. First, he let everybody hold him again. Then he tossed him lightly into the air. Hooty lurched a little, then caught himself, and, flapping his strong, noiseless wings, flew off into the twilight.

"Good-by, Hooty!" Flora called after him.

"Come again sometime!" Peter shouted.

"He will." Pudge was sure of that. And ever after, when he caught sight of gray ghostlike wings swooping around the barn at twilight, he always said, "Here comes Hooty."

And nobody could prove that he wasn't right!

Chapter 3

Thank You, Midget Mouse

It had rained for three days in a row. Rain spilled against the windows steadily, as if it never meant to stop. The big Buttonwood kitchen, usually so cheerful, began to look a little bedraggled, with wet coats steaming on chairs, boots set beside the wood box, books and toys scattered here and there, and the six young Buttonwoods sandwiched in between.

"I'm fed up with rain," Pudge said frankly. "Just cooped up inside all day except for times when I splash out to the barn to help with the chores—well, it's kind of boring after the first day or two."

"Yeah—I wish we could go for a hike or something," Flora admitted.

19

Betsy stopped rocking and looked up from *Pilgrim's Progress,* which she was reading for the tenth time.

"Why don't you read?" she offered helpfully. "That's what rainy days are for, isn't it, Mom?"

Before Mom had a chance to answer, Crish bobbed up from her place on the floor, where she was playing a game of Uncle Wiggley with Peter.

"You can play with us," she said eagerly. "We wouldn't mind having you help, would we, Pete?"

"Well, I guess not!" Pudge said firmly. "That's baby stuff for sure. You don't catch me—"

Peter jumped up, too. "You think you're so smart, Pudge Buttonwood! Well, let me tell you—"

He moved a step backward, tripped over his erector set, and sat down hard. Instead of getting up again, he lay there, howling.

"Are you hurt, Peter?" Mom asked anxiously.

"No, it isn't that," Peter gulped. "It's Midget. He's gone."

"Oh, no!" Mom gasped while the rest all groaned.

"The next time he disappears, we're going to set a trap," Flora warned.

But Peter paid no attention to her. He knew that Midget Mouse was safe. After all, Mom and Dad had said he could keep him.

But catching Midget again was quite a job. Pudge discovered him on the wood box and sneaked over there, while everybody else held his breath. Slowly, carefully, he reached toward him.

"There!" Pudge said—but his hand was empty. A minute later, Betsy caught a glimpse of Midget, sitting on the clock shelf, calmly combing his whiskers.

Finally, Peter did manage to sneak up on Midget as he perched on the arm of Mom's rocker. With a quick grab, Peter had him. After that, the Buttonwoods sat down for a moment's rest.

"Just the same—I'm tired of rain," Pudge said after a bit.

"Shall I let Midget stir things up again?" Peter demanded with a grin.

"You'd better hang on to that creature, or I'll feed him to the cats," Pudge warned.

Peter bristled up right away. "You won't either! You just leave my mouse alone, or—"

"Boys!" Mom said.

"Well, he's always picking on me," Peter muttered.

"Pete can't take a speck of teasing, either," Pudge complained.

"Just remember—'It takes two to make a quarrel,'" Mom reminded them. "Now, before you get to bickering just because you're bored, I have a suggestion."

They all looked at Mom suspiciously. Was she going to give them a job they hated, to keep them from griping again?

"You could all adjourn to the little attic, where last year's hickory nuts are stored," she said. "If you crack and pick out enough nuts, Betsy can make a batch of fudge."

With a whoop that could be heard at the barn, they agreed. It was a suggestion that suited them all.

"Better take a chunk of wood and the hammer," Mom reminded them.

"Yes, and a pan for the nut meats," Betsy added.

"And some nails to use for nutpicks," Crish said.

"Plus an old rug to catch the trash," Mom told them.

Loaded down like that, they all trooped up the back stairs. The little attic wasn't really an attic at all; it was simply a storeroom, behind the back bedroom. But it was the only attic the Buttonwoods had; so they always called it that.

It was good to get out of the kitchen for a bit. Rain drummed on the sloping roof of the back part of the attic (over the lean-to woodshed), but it didn't sound quite so doleful now. Pudge cracked hickory nuts galore, while the rest worked away with their nail nutpicks.

"Remember the fun we had picking up these nuts last fall?" Flora asked dreamily.

That started them off, and they spent a long time talking over past adventures—hikes and picnics and so on.

"I hope we go nutting again this year," Betsy said. "It's always such fun—"

All of a sudden, Peter threw himself on the floor and began to howl. The rest all turned to stare.

"What's the matter now, Peter Buttonwood?" Betsy demanded severely. "You're getting to be a regular crybaby."

"It's Midget," Peter wailed, "He's gone!"

The three older Buttonwoods looked at each other. It was Flora who finally said what they were all thinking.

"We'll try our best, Pete, but I'm not sure we can catch him again, up here."

Pudge nodded his head. "He may be gone for good this time." Then, seeing Peter's face, he added, "But we'll do our best before we give up, anyway."

It was a job for sure—trying to catch one little mouse among so many boxes and trunks. Once in a while, as they pulled things around, they did catch a flicker of a tail or the shadow of a sharp nose, but each time, Midget was gone before they could capture him. Betsy finally crawled 'way under the eaves, pulling away boxes as she went.

"Ah-choo! My, but it's dusty back here," she complained. "I bet it's been ages since some of these boxes were opened. Oh, there he is! I see him. Now, just a minute—"

Betsy leaned forward. Slowly, slowly, she put out her hand, but just as it closed, Midget whisked away again. The others groaned.

"It's okay," Betsy said cheerfully. "He was too smart this time. I saw him dive right into this box; so Mr. Midget is as good as caught already."

"Let's just take the whole box down to the kitchen," Pudge

said. "Crish, you bring the nuts. I think I've cracked enough, and we can finish picking them out down there, while Betsy gets the fudge started."

Mom looked up when they all came trooping down again. "Finished already?" she asked.

Pudge explained about Midget. "And he's right in this box; so get set to grab, everybody!"

The Buttonwoods formed a circle around Pudge. They leaned forward as he slowly, slowly lifted the lid. It wasn't till he stirred the contents of the box that Midget, with a sudden squeak, appeared on the edge. Two seconds later, he was safe in Peter's pocket.

"I see a book in here," Pudge said, as he rummaged around in the box.

"Let me see!" Betsy was at his elbow right away. "Why, it's a copy of *Little Men,* Mom. Where in the world did it come from?"

"Here are a couple of little men—real ones, I mean," Crish said. "They feel just as smooth as glass, Mom. Where—"

"My little ivory chessmen—and the book from Alfred Underhill," Mom said. "Why, I haven't thought of them for years."

She sat down on her rocker with the chessmen and *Little Men* on her lap. There was a faraway kind of look on her face.

"Tell us about it—will you, Mom?" Betsy begged. "We can all be picking out nut meats while you talk."

Mom rocked gently back and forth, back and forth. She held the ivory chessmen in her hands as she began her story.

"When I was a little girl, just Peter's age, we lived near the Underhill house," she said. "It was big and fine, with lace curtains at the windows. I used to stand at the gate and look in—and wonder what it was like inside."

Crish gave an excited wiggle. "It sounds just like a book, Mom!"

"Then, one day Mr. Underhill came to our house and asked whether my older sister, Martha, could come and work for him."

"Did she go?" Peter demanded.

"Now, don't you twins keep interrupting!" Pudge said.

Mom waited until they got quiet, then went on.

"Grandma and Grandpa talked it over for a long time, and they finally decided to let Martha go. One day, Grandma sent me over to the house with a message for her."

Crish opened her mouth to interrupt, but Pudge caught her eye and shook his head. She made a face at him, but at least, she didn't say anything out loud.

"That house was like a dream," Mom went on. "Martha took me through it. There were velvet draperies behind the lace curtains and thick carpets, so that you didn't make any noise at all when you walked. The furniture was big and heavy and the walls were just lined with portraits of sober-faced men and stiff-looking women. That was the day I first met Alfred."

"You mean he lived there?" Peter burst out.

"Yes. He was Mr. Underhill's son. The mother died when Alfred was a baby, so he and his father lived alone in that big house. It was very sad, really. Because Alfred had every-thing—toys and books and clothes—everything except the love and companionship he needed most."

The Buttonwoods looked at each other. No mom! No brothers and sisters! They simply couldn't imagine what that would be like.

"I wonder what he did on rainy days?" Pudge said soberly.

"Did you go to play with him sometimes, after that, Mom?" Betsy asked.

Mom nodded. "Yes, we became very good friends. But he liked best to come to our house to play—he always said we could have more fun there than at his home. He gave me the little chessmen and the book just before he and his father moved away to another community."

They all waited, hoping to hear more, but Mom shook her head. "No, I never saw or heard of him again. I've wondered sometimes what ever became of him. I always remembered him as a lonely little boy, without a mother."

Then Mom became her bustling self again. "Put the chess-men in the corner cupboard in the dining room," she said to Flora. "Betsy, you may have the book to read, then put it in the bookcase with the others. Right now, you'd better get started with that candy."

The rain spilled down the windowpanes, as fast as before, but the Buttonwood kitchen had suddenly regained its cheerfulness. Betsy flaxed around, measuring sugar into a saucepan, while Crish gathered up the nut meats and then dumped the shells into the coal pail.

The Buttonwoods all felt cheerful, too. They had each other and Mom and Dad. What, after all, was a little rain? The thought of that lonely little boy of long ago made them suddenly realize how much they loved and needed each other.

As soon as the fudge was finished, they all settled down again. Betsy picked up *Little Men* and plunked down on Mom's rocker.

"Let's read a while," she suggested.

She looked around at the little circle of intent faces. At the edge of Peter's pocket, she caught a sudden glimpse of a tiny whiskered face.

"Peter Buttonwood, you'd better hang on to that mouse!" she said.

Peter grinned around at them all. "Well, I don't see why you make such a fuss," he said. "After all, who was it that discovered that box? It isn't every day we have the fun we've had today. I vote we say thank you to Midget."

The rest laughed, of course, but they all agreed with Peter just the same.

Chapter 4

Buttonwood Playhouse

Pudge and Betsy were busy, trying to catch the pullets in the brooder house.

"Whew!" Pudge mopped his hot forehead with a big red hanky. He looked at the three pullets, huddled in a crate set just outside the door. Then he turned to stare at the dozens of other pullets still enjoying their freedom.

"It will take us forever to do this job, Betsy," he complained. "Look at those stupid chickens—don't they know they'll like being on range a lot better than being cooped up in here?"

Betsy mopped her face, too. Her sleeve had a three-corner-ed tear in it, where (as she told Mom afterward) a nail reach-ed right out and grabbed her as she dashed past.

29

"Chickens don't have much sense, really," she admitted. "But I think there must be a better way of doing this, Pudge. Maybe the twins and Flo would help—"

"They won't like it," Pudge predicted darkly. "I can just hear the howls already. And with Mom and Dad both gone, I kind of hate to start anything."

But Betsy refused to give up. "You know what Mom always says," she told Pudge. " 'Where there's a will, there's a way.' And I think we ought to be able to think of a way to make them want to help. Oh, Pudge! I know what! Why, it will be just the thing!"

"Well, it will have to be good," Pudge said doubtfully.

Just then, Peter's tousled head appeared around a corner of the brooder house. "Flo says dinner is ready," he announced. "An' I'm starving; so come on right now."

"Sh! Don't say anything to him," Betsy whispered to Pudge.

As they turned to go, Pudge caught a glimpse of a whiskered face at the edge of a stone pile nearby. "Hey, Pete!" he yelled. "There goes Midget!"

But Peter refused to let himself be worried. By slipping his hand into his pocket, he could tell that Midget Mouse was safe enough. "Maybe that's Midget's cousin," he said with a grin.

At the dinner table Betsy brought up her big idea again. "What would you think of using the brooder house for a playhouse this summer, while it's empty?" she asked.

The others stopped eating to stare at her. "It's awfully

dirty," Flora said. "I don't think we could get it clean enough."

"But we always do scrub it down, right after the pullets are moved," Betsy said. "We could just do a little extra work, and I'm sure it would be all right."

Pudge leaned on one elbow on the table. (Since Mom wasn't there to remind him, he got by with it, too!) "You know, if we got it fixed up right, it would be a good place for my collection."

The others all laughed. Pudge's collection was strewn all over the house, and the rest always chuckled when he mentioned it.

"It might be worth the work just to get rid of it in here," Betsy told him. "There's that table in the woodshed. It looks awful, with paint spilled over it, but it's good and solid and I know Mom would let us have it."

"And I could move all my dolls out there," Flora said.

"If Pudge or Dad would build a shelf across one end, we could use that for a dollhouse."

"And we could use some of those bricks at the bottom of the pasture and put some boards across for bookshelves," Betsy put in. "I could move my books out there. And—if you'd build a little three-cornered shelf across one corner. I could use it for a desk, Pudge. Oh, that would really be something!"

By then, they were all planning together. "We could move our Uncle Wiggley game out there," Crish said. "Then on rainy days Mom wouldn't have to step over us every time she moved."

"And I could keep my erector set out there," Peter added. "Then I could leave it set up all the time—even on Sunday."

"Well, what are we waiting for?" Pudge demanded. "If we hurry up and get those pullets moved, I think Dad will help us clean it out as soon as he gets back with the feed—before he goes over to Granddad's for Mom and Small Susie."

Then, what a bustle and scramble there was! Quickly, Betsy scraped the dishes and set them in the sink, while Flora took the butter to the cellar and tucked the bread into a lard can. For once, nobody complained about whose turn it was— they all just pitched in and helped.

As they started down through Little Orchard, Pudge saw Peter put his hand into his pocket. "You'd better leave Midget at home," he said. "If he gets away during this adventure, he'll be gone for good, you know."

But Peter shook his head, "Midget likes fun, too. An' I know he gets dull, sitting around in his box, while we're out doing things."

Pudge gave up, with a shrug of his shoulders. "Okay. He's your mouse."

With all of them working together, they had the pullets out of there in a hurry. When the last one was shut up in the range shelters, they hurried back to the house to wait for Dad. After a bit, he drove in with the old truck. They were sitting on the porch drinking lemonade. He listened to their story with a twinkle in his eye.

"And we moved all the pullets," Peter said importantly. "Some of 'em squawked like anything when we caught 'em, too."

"We cooped them up in the range shelters, just as you said," Crish added. "By tomorrow morning, they'll feel at home in their new houses—"

"Then they won't all come trooping back to our playhouse when we let them out," Flora finished.

Dad finished his lemonade and set the glass on the porch railing. "Your playhouse! Since when?"

They could all tell that he was teasing, though. "Since about noon today, or a little after," Pudge told him with a wink.

"We kind of thought you might want to clean it out before you go for Mom, then we could start scrubbing," Betsy hinted.

Dad threw up his hands. "I see you have everything planned; so I might as well give in," he said with a grin. "If a few sturdy boys would like to help me, it would go faster."

Pudge and Peter both jumped to their feet.

"I'm your man, Dad," Pudge said.

"What about the girls?" Peter demanded. "They oughta help too."

"Don't worry, Pete. We'll do our share when it comes to scrubbing," Betsy promised.

And she kept her promise, too. As soon as Dad and the boys finished, she took a broom and started. The rest all trailed after her, and it wasn't long until each one had a bucket and was carrying water from the pump in the washhouse.

"It doesn't seem long since we first got those baby chicks, does it?" said Flora, putting her pail down just outside the door to wait until Betsy needed the water. "And now they're pullets already."

"Yeah," Pudge agreed. "And it takes us forever to grow up—forever!"

"Remember how they all came in a box?" Peter said. "They cheeped like anything when Dad carried them out here."

"And then he had to dip their beaks into water to teach them to drink," Flora added.

"Chicks drink in a funny way, don't they?" Crish put in. "Like this."

She put her face down, took a drink out of a nearby bucket, then put her head 'way back so that the water could run down her throat.

Flora had a sudden idea. "Let's all be chicks," she said.

In a minute, they were all hopping around in the grass, chirping loudly. Whenever they passed the water bucket, they stopped for a drink, chick style. When Peter put back his head, flapped his wings, and gave a squeaky crow, they all shouted.

Then, Pudge saw Peter's hand going into his pocket. He

knew by his face what had happened, even before Peter threw back his head and began to howl.

"That's a funny noise for a chick,'" he said. "Now, come on and cut it out, Pete. If Midget's gone, we'll help you hunt for him, but carrying on like that won't do a speck of good."

When Betsy came out to check on her water supply she heard the whole story. She shook her head a little, while a line creased her forehead.

"We'll try, Pete, but remember we can't promise. Outdoors is a pretty big place and Midget is just one little mouse."

And they all did hunt, for quite a while. The longer they looked, the more sober Peter's face became.

"Oh, dear! What in this world will we do?" Betsy whispered, as she passed close to Pudge in her search. "Say, Pudge. Remember those wood mice we saw this forenoon, over near the stone pile?"

Pudge gave Betsy a long look. Then, suddenly, he caught on.

"It wouldn't have to be the same mouse—he'd never know the difference," Betsy added.

Pudge nodded his head. Then, he began to circle farther and farther, and each circle brought him nearer to the stone pile. Long practice in catching Midget helped him as he moved a stone and made a quick grab. Without a word, he carried the little wood mouse back to Peter.

"I'd go put him in his box right quick," he said. "And

maybe you'd better keep him penned up for a couple of days until he—well, kind of gets over his scare a little."

Betsy and Pudge both looked worried, but Peter didn't suspect a thing. He just took Midget and ran off as fast as he could.

The rest of the afternoon went by without a single mishap, unless you count the time Flora tripped and upset a whole pail of water all over herself. Or the time Crish screamed because she saw a little garter snake slithering through the grass. When she told Peter about it, he said, "Where was it, Crish? Do tell me, quick!"

Then he spent a long time looking all through the grass for it.

"It's no use, anyway, Pete," Pudge said. "You know Mom would never let you keep it."

"Well, I hope not!" Flora said with a shudder.

But it was days before the playhouse was really finished. They spent hours and hours fixing it up. Pudge brought his tools and made shelves here and there as directed—one along one wall for Flora's dolls and Peter's erector set, and another across the corner for Betsy's desk. Mom helped Betsy dye feed bags a lovely shade of pink. Then she and Flora sewed curtains for the windows.

When Grandma heard about the playhouse, she gave them an old rug for the floor. And Aunt Erma donated an old rocker. It really looked pretty, after Betsy made a cover for it with some of the pink feed bags, but they always had to be careful not to lean back too far, or over it went!

"Oh, Mom—isn't it splendid?" Betsy asked one day when Mom came to visit the playhouse.

Mom nodded her head. "And you've all worked hard, too."

"Oh, it was fun," Flora said.

"It sure was," Peter added.

Pudge and Betsy looked at each other. They were remembering the day they moved the pullets.

"It really was," Betsy said slowly. She sounded surprised.

"The things we do together are always fun." Pudge said that as if he were just finding it out.

Mom smiled around at them all. "That's right. And now I wonder how many Buttonwoods would be in favor of an all-of-us-together picnic supper in the playhouse this evening?"

They all shouted, "I am!" so loudly that Mom held her hands over her ears.

"I guess we're all agreed then," she said smiling. "And now, I'd suggest that you help lug things down here right now."

And, laughing and talking, they all trooped up to the house after her.

Chapter 5

Books for Betsy

"But, Mom!" Betsy protested. "I don't want to go—not this week, anyway. The bookmobile is coming to Satterlie's store on Wednesday, and it comes only once a month, you know."

"I'm sorry," Mom said. Her forehead creased into a worried frown. "But, Betsy, Grandma Buttonwood needs you right now."

"Why can't Flora go?"

Mom shook her head. "With Grandma flat in bed? Hardly! Why, she'd have to do all the cooking and see to it that Grandma takes her medicine and everything—I'm afraid Flora isn't quite up to that."

Betsy looked down at the scuffed toes of her worn brown

oxfords. She didn't want to go—not the least little bit. But Mom was right. They couldn't send Flora.

"Okay—I guess I'll have to go," she agreed finally.

Yet she couldn't help feeling a little sorry for herself as she went upstairs to pack. After all, it wasn't fair. She had to give up her plans just because Flora was too scatterbrained to go. Why, you were really better off if you weren't steady and dependable—

"Hurry up, Betsy Buttonwood," Crish called from the foot of the stairs. "You're keeping Granddad waiting."

"Let him wait," Betsy muttered to herself, but she slammed the suitcase shut and dashed downstairs.

"I'll take your books back to the bookmobile, Betsy," Flora promised.

"Okay," Betsy said briefly.

She wasn't really worried about the books that needed to be returned. What really counted were the ones she had wanted to check out for herself—three in all. Now it would be a whole month before she'd have another chance!

"Maybe there are some books at Granddad Buttonwood's," Mom said. "There used to be, I remember—when they lived in the farmhouse. They were stored in that bookcase above Granddad's desk."

Betsy shook her head. "I've looked through all of those. They're just awful! Nothing less than a hundred years old, and not a storybook among 'em, either."

Mom wasn't convinced. "There used to be—I'm sure of that. You just look again, dear. And be sure to take good care of Grandma. I won't worry about her while you're there.

"Betsy, Granddad's waiting," Crish reminded her again.

She ran out and climbed into his car quickly, then turned to wave good-by to the rest of the Buttonwoods. They were all lined up in the side yard—Mom, holding Small Sue, Dad, the twins, who were giggling as usual, Pudge, and Flora. Behind them was the big gray Buttonwood farmhouse that hadn't had a coat of paint since Betsy could remember, with the garden and Little Orchard just beyond. The very last thing she saw as they turned down the road was Dad's big red hanky. Pudge had grabbed it and was waving like mad.

The work at Granddad Buttonwood's wasn't so hard, really. Betsy cooked meals and washed dishes and cleaned the house, just as she did at home, but she had to do everything on her own here. She saw to it that Grandma took her pills right on time and tried to amuse her by talking or reading whenever she was awake.

However, Grandma took a long nap every afternoon. Time seemed to creep for Betsy then. She went into the big front parlor, where an old-fashioned upright organ nudged elbows with a queer, scratchy kind of sofa, and tried to find a book to read, but without much luck. Wednesday afternoon was worst of all, because she kept thinking about the bookmobile.

"Oh, dear—you'd think Granddad's would have at least one

storybook," she thought, running her fingers along the shelves. "*Edifying Sermons*—they look as dull as the title sounds. I might like them fifty years from now. *The Hartzler Family*— why, that isn't a thing but long lists of names. Here's an old German songbook, a commentary, and two concordances. No, there isn't a thing here that I'd enjoy the least bit."

Just then the clock in the front hall struck the hour—bong, bong, bong. Three o'clock! Just the time the bookmobile would be pulling in at Satterlie's store. Betsy leaned her chin on her hand and stared out through the window at the patterns the sunshine made on the porch floor where it peeked through the cinnamon vine.

"I'd be over there waiting for it if I were at home," she thought dolefully. "I'd spend the whole hour it stays there on my knees in front of the shelves, just leafing through book after book. If I couldn't find any new ones that I liked, I'd reread *Little Women* or *Heidi*, maybe. Oh, dear!"

Just when Betsy was beginning to think she couldn't stand the silence another minute, she heard a rap at the back door. She slipped out to answer it, hoping Grandma wouldn't hear.

"Why, come right in, Aunt Erma," Betsy whispered. "Grandma's asleep, but—"

"Oh, no, I'm not," Grandma called from the bedroom. "I'm wide awake right this minute; so come on in, Erma."

"I hate to bother you at a time like this," Aunt Erma said to Grandma, "but the Sewing meets tomorrow, you know."

Grandma nodded her head. "That's right! And I forgot to hunt out those quilt patterns for you."

"Don't worry about it the least bit," Aunt Erma began.

"Could I find them for you, Grandma?" Betsy broke in. "I'd be glad to try if you want me to."

"Well," Grandma said, "they're up in the attic and I'm not sure just where. In one of those cardboard boxes under the front eaves, I think."

"I'll find them if they're there. Then Granddad can bring them over to you this evening, Aunt Erma."

As Betsy started upstairs she heard Aunt Erma say, "Are you sure I can depend on Betsy, Grandma? We'll need those patterns tomorrow—"

"Of course you can," Grandma said. "You can always depend on Betsy, Erma. You'll never know what a comfort it's been to me to know that."

Betsy went on slowly. There was something to be said for being dependable—something about the way you felt inside. Even if it didn't always seem to pay off!

"Whew! Is it ever hot up here!" She said out loud as she began to paw through box after box. She found old clothes, Grandma's carpet rags, boxes of letters yellow with age, empty quart jars, tag ends of paint in little cans, jar lids, and even rubber rings tied into neat bundles with string.

"Well, I hope this is it—or I'm afraid I will melt," Betsy thought as she pulled a big box out to the middle of the floor.

She caught sight of herself in a big mirror propped against the wall. Her face was streaked with dust and a blackened cobweb draped down over her brown braids and looped itself over one ear.

"Oh, dear! I do look a sight! But maybe this box is the one."

And, sure enough, it was. Right on top were quilt patterns of all kinds. Some were tucked into dingy envelopes. Others had been placed carefully between the pages of old magazines. Under them—

Betsy drew in her breath sharply. There, beneath the patterns, were stacks of books, old and tattered.

"But these are storybooks," Betsy said.

She pulled out one after another—*Aunt Martha's Corner Cupboard, The Little Colonel's House Party, Tom Brown's School Days,* and a calico-covered *Appleton's Fifth Reader* with the date in front—September 12, 1881.

"This belonged to Elizabeth Buttonwood—I wonder who she was?" Betsy thought. "Oh, isn't this simply super—all the books I want to read right here!"

She grabbed the quilt patterns and dashed downstairs.

"There's a box of books up there, too! Did you know that, Grandma?"

"Why, yes, of course. We packed those away when we left the farm, Betsy."

"May I bring them down to read, please?" Betsy asked. "I'd like to, if you don't mind."

"Why, certainly. I should have brought them down long ago, but I forgot that they were up there. In fact, Betsy," Grandma went on with a smile, "I really think those books should go home with you as a thank-you gift for all you've done this week. I'm feeling ever so much better and it's because you've taken such good care of me, I'm sure."

Betsy kissed Grandma. Then she ran upstairs and brought

an armload of books down to the kitchen. No more lonely times at Granddad's now! Best of all, she'd get to take them home with her afterward. And if Grandma kept getting better, she'd be going soon, too.

She opened a battered copy of *Pilgrim's Progress* and began to read, but just then the big clock struck the hour again—bong, bong, bong, bong, bong.

"Five o'clock. Oh, bother!"

For a moment, she hestitated. It was time for Grandma's medicine, and after that she'd have to get supper. And she did so want to read at least a little.

"But if I hadn't been dependable, Grandma never would have sent me up to the attic in the first place," she thought. "And I never would have found these books at all."

"And you wouldn't feel half as good, either," something deep inside reminded her.

Betsy dropped *Pilgrim's Progress* in a hurry. Then she went in to Grandma, smiling.

"Time for your pills again," she said. "And then—well, how about some chicken soup for supper? My own special brand, that is. You can call it Betsy's Best."

Chapter 6

Mom Buttonwood's Birthday

Pudge dropped over the rail fence into Little Ochard where the other Buttonwood children were busy picking up some early apples.

"Say," he said soberly. "Do you realize what day tomorrow is?"

"It's Wednesday, isn't it?" Crish said.

"What are you talking about, Pudge?" Flora demanded.

Betsy straightened up slowly and rubbed her back. "Tomorrow? It's July 24—"

She stopped and they all looked at each other.

"July 24!" Flora gasped.

"Yeah—July 24." Pudge kicked a half-rotten apple and sent

it smashing against a tree trunk nearby. "Mom's birthday. And not a one of us has a present for her."

"And no money to buy presents, either," Crish wailed.

"And no way of getting to town, even if we did have the money," Flora added.

"Maybe we could make something for her," Peter suggested.

Pudge shook his head. "Not something she really wants. There isn't time."

"Something the matter over there?" a voice behind them at them from beyond the fence. "Say! You youngsters do look asked mildly. They turned to see Dad Buttonwood grinning glum. Can I help?"

"It's Mom's birthday," Pudge explained.

"We forgot all about it until this minute," Peter admitted.

"And now we don't have a thing for her—and no money to buy anything—and no way of getting to town, even if we had the money." Flora was really piling up troubles.

"And it's too late to make anything," Crish added.

Dad leaned against the fence and brushed across a clump of ragweed with one hand. "Suppose you did have money. And some way of getting to town. What would you buy Mom for her birthday?" he asked.

"Oh, a hanky or something," Pudge said vaguely.

"Candy, maybe," Crish suggested.

"I don't know," Betsy admitted honestly. "It's always hard for me to pick out presents."

"Well, my guess is you could give Mom something she'd like a lot without going off the place or spending a cent."

"Oh, Dad!" They all said together, like a chorus.

"I mean it. The size of a present doesn't really depend on how much money you spend. Why don't you try to find out what Mom really wants. I may be mistaken, but I have a feeling it will be something that won't cost you a cent."

Dad walked off then, leaving them standing there to talk things over.

"But how could we find out?" Pudge asked.

"Say—I've got an idea," Betsy said. "You know that story in one of our books about the three wishes? Why don't we bring it up—pretend we're just in fun—and find out what Mom wants that way?"

"Sounds all right to me," Flora agreed. "Let's try it as soon as we take these apples in."

"You'd better get a move on, too." Pudge said. "Mom was wondering why you were staying so long."

"Well, I like that!" Crish was indignant. "Now you tell us!"

"I didn't want you marching off before I had a chance to talk things over," Pudge explained. "Here, I'll help. Give me that basket. You and Betsy carry the other one between you."

Back in the kitchen, Mom looked up from her ironing. "You certainly took your time," she said. "Hurry and quarter a pan of apples for apple sauce and get them on the stove. I'll need room to cook dinner before long."

"I'll wash the apples," Pudge offered. "We can save time that way." He filled the dishpan and set it under the pump.

"I was reading a story the other day." Betsy said, offhand like, as she picked up a paring knife and got busy. "In it, a fairy told a man he could have three wishes. Anything in the whole world, mind you."

"I wish a fairy would tell me that," Flora sighed. "I'd wish for a million dollars right off."

Mom looked up quickly. "Let's hope not! Dear me, child. What would you do with a million dollars?"

"Well, what would you wish for if you had three wishes, Mom?" Betsy asked. The other Buttonwoods held their breath, waiting for her answer. Crish giggled in that I-know-a-secret kind of way, but the rest frowned her to silence.

"Me?" Mom looked surprised. Then her eyes began to twinkle. "First thing, I'd wish every weed out of the garden."

The children all looked guilty at that. Mom had been after them time and again about that garden, but they kept putting it off!

"What else, Mom?" Flora asked.

"Well, let me see." Mom put down her iron and pulled out another of Crish's dresses. "I'd wish (and her eyes fell on her workbasket, piled high with socks, as usual) that those socks were as whole as they were the day they first left the store. Oh, yes—and I'd also wish for a whole day to visit with Grandma, without having to worry about getting meals or anything."

As soon as they could get away, the little Buttonwoods sneaked off to the far end of the woodshed.

"Dad was right," Pudge said.

"He sure was," Flora agreed ruefully.

"You know—we could make those wishes come true," Betsy said suddenly. "Every one of them."

"How?" Peter demanded. His eyes got big.

"If Dad would take Mom to Grandpa's tomorrow," Betsy began.

The others caught on right away. "We could stay home and weed the garden," Pudge said.

"And do the mending," Flora added.

They stood there for a long minute, thinking things over. Then Pudge walked over toward the garden and the rest followed.

"Look at all those weeds!" Betsy gave a long sigh.

"There sure are a lot of 'em," Peter said.

Pudge shook his head. "It's going to be an all-day job, I'm afraid."

"And then there'll be those stockings, too," Flora pointed out. "And I do hate to darn. Besides, no matter how hard I try, my darns will get bunchy, anyway."

Then Crish spoke up suddenly. "But if that's what Mom really wants for her birthday, we ought to do it for her," she said. "Besides, I think it would be fun to surprise her."

"But how would we explain to Mom about us not going to

Grandpa's, too?" Flora objected. "She'd know something was up—or else, she'd think we were all sick."

"But, Flora—you know 'where there's a will, there's a way.' " Crish sounded so exactly like Mom as she said that, that the rest just roared.

"I know!" Pudge said, after they quieted down a bit. "We'd have to ask Dad to help us."

Then Betsy had an inspiration. "He could say that he thought she needed a vacation from us, too, and insist that we all stay at home."

"And we could tell her we don't mind, because we have plans of our own! I really think that would work, without making Mom feel bad or worry about us," Pudge said.

So that's how it happened that Mom and Dad Buttonwood drove down the lane the next morning, minus all the little Buttonwoods except Small Sue. As soon as they were gone, the left-behinds got busy. Oh, how they all flew around!

"If Pudge and the twins would work on the garden, Flo and I could get started on those socks," Betsy said.

"I know," Pudge said to his two helpers. "I'll run the wheel hoe between the rows while you weed. Then, when that's done, I'll help with the weeding, too."

"That's right," Betsy added. "You know, we'll have to work like mad or we won't get it finished before Mom gets home tonight."

After that, for a long while, they were too busy to talk very

much. On the side porch, needles flew in and out, in and out, while in the garden, the heap of weeds grew bigger and bigger. Finally, Pudge had to stop long enough to get the wheelbarrow and haul some of them away.

"Why don't you make some lemonade, Betsy?" he called as he flew past. "I'm telling you, it's really hot out there."

"Okay," Betsy agreed. And a few minutes later, she called them in for tall glasses of cold lemonade.

"Oooh! Is that ever good!" Crish said, gulping hers down.

"Say! You girls sure have it soft," Peter said. "Just sitting around in the shade. You ought to see what it's like to work out there in the garden."

Betsy and Flora looked at each other.

"We'll trade for a bit, if you want to," Flora said with a wink at Betsy.

"Not me!" Pudge said firmly.

But Crish and Peter were ready for anything.

"Sure, I know how to darn socks," Peter said. "I've seen Mom do it and it looks real easy."

"Me, too," Crish added. "It isn't a bit hard. I know, even if I never really tried myself."

Betsy looked at Flora over the twins' heads. "It won't last long," she whispered. So she and Flora went with Pudge to work in the garden, while the twins stayed on the porch. In about half an hour, Betsy went to check on them. They were both struggling away, but they looked nearly as hot and bothered as they did when they first came in from the garden. Crish had her mouth puckered up as she tried to untangle her thread, and Peter was sucking his thumb, where he'd jabbed it with his needle. They both jumped up as soon as they saw Betsy.

"I'm rested now," Crish announced. "Somehow, weeds don't make me as tired as needles do."

"Me, too," Peter agreed. "Besides, we're kind of slow at this, Betsy. Maybe you and Flo had better work on it again, so it will be finished in time."

Betsy and Flora waited until the twins were back in the garden, then they leaned against the porch railing and laughed and laughed. The queer puckered places in those socks were just too funny. Just the same, they were careful not to laugh too loud, because they didn't want to hurt Crish's and Peter's feelings.

The rest of the day simply whizzed by. At noon, the Buttonwoods stopped for a few bites of lunch, then went right back to work again. By late afternoon the twins lagged a little, but Betsy and Flora had finished the last of the socks, so they could help with the weeding then.

Suddenly, the last bit of work was done. Fingers were sore and backs ached, but they hardly noticed. The clock on the shelf in the kitchen struck four.

"Dad and Mom ought to be home soon," Pudge said.

"Hey—I think I hear them now," Peter added.

Crish ran to the window. "That's right—there they come!"

A few minutes later, the big kitchen was full of talk and laughter.

"Remember those three wishes you made yesterday, Mom?" Betsy asked.

Mom nodded her head. Then she smiled at Dad. "I wished for a day at Grandpa's, and that came true in a hurry, didn't it?"

"Maybe a fairy overheard you," Dad said. He sounded as if he meant what he said, but the others caught a twinkle in his eyes.

"Well, Dad would make a pretty outsized fairy, I think,"

Pudge said with a chuckle.

"Anyway, your other wishes came true, too," Crish said, grabbing Mom's hand.

"See—there's your mending basket and it's empty," Flora added.

Mom rubbed her eyes, as if she couldn't quite believe what she saw. Then she looked at the stack of neatly mended socks nearby.

"Why, my dears!" she said.

"And the garden's weeded, too," Peter told her. "Just come and look. There's not a single weed as big as your thumb anywhere in it."

Of course, Mom had to hug them all at the same time. Then she went to look and exclaim over the garden with its long straight rows and not a weed anywhere.

"Why, I do think this is the happiest birthday I've ever had," she said with a queer catch in her breath.

She hugged Crish again and dropped a kiss on top of Peter's tousled head. The three older Buttonwoods looked at each other in sudden understanding.

They knew it wasn't just the garden and the mending and the visit to Grandpa's. Giving Mom what she wanted, even if it was hard, and doing it simply because they loved her—that was what really counted. They didn't know just why, but deep down inside they felt just as happy as Mom looked.

Chapter 7

Treasure Hunt

The three oldest Buttonwoods sat on the front-porch railing, like so many crows in a row, swinging their feet and talking. They were discussing a book they'd been reading, called *The Treasure Seekers.*

"I just wish we'd have adventures the way those Bastable youngsters did," Pudge said with a sigh. "Oh, we wouldn't be silly enough to get into some of the scrapes they did, but they really had fun."

"One thing I noticed," Betsy said thoughtfully. "Those children got into all kinds of mischief, but they never meant to. In the beginning, they always started out to do something nice for somebody, but then it turned out all wrong."

"I noticed that, too." Flora shook her head. "That's different from us. When we're bad, we usually do it on purpose."

"Not always," Pudge objected. "We don't just make up our minds—now, today we're going to be bad, no matter what. Usually some little thing starts us off. Like that business about the bonfire."

"I do wish you wouldn't keep bringing up things like that, Pudge," Flo complained. "It makes me feel creepy, just thinking about it."

"I never before saw Dad look the way he did then," Betsy said.

"And I hope I never do again," Flora admitted. "Just the same, I think we walked into that with our eyes open. We knew we weren't supposed to have matches, even if they did fall out of Mr. Broadwater's pockets."

"Well, anyway—I wish something exciting would happen to us for a change. Those book children are always doing interesting things." Pudge kicked the railing discontentedly. "Seems like something happened to them at least once a week, while we just go on in the same old rut forever."

"Well, why don't you go and hunt some adventure instead of sitting here on the porch, expecting them to come to you?" Mom said from the screen door behind them. "'The grass always looks greener on the other side of the fence,' you know."

The Buttonwoods whirled around in a hurry.

"We didn't hear you, Mom!"

"No fair—sneaking up on us like that!"

But Mom shook her head. "If you want to talk secrets, then don't do it at the top of your voice, right outside the bedroom window where I'm trying to get Susie to sleep. You all know better than that."

Pudge and Betsy and Flora looked at each other.

"Oh, dear!" was all Betsy could say.

"We forgot, Mom. Honest we did," Flora told her.

"It's so dull around here, we have to keep talking," Pudge protested. "If we had something exciting to do, we wouldn't hang around the house, waking the baby."

"I was just planning to suggest something," Mom said.

They held their breath. Suppose Mom said weed onions or hoe sweet corn or pick peas? In a minute she went on, and they breathed again.

"You were talking about the adventures those Bastable children had when they went treasure hunting. Well, why don't you go treasure hunting, too? There's a treasure in our lower pasture right now, that you might want to look for."

"Really?" Betsy sounded as if she didn't quite believe Mom.

"What kind of treasure?" Flo demanded.

"Like that money Uncle dropped into the place where the Bastables were digging, I suppose," Pudge said.

But Mom shook her head, smiling. "I didn't put it there. Neither did Dad. But we know that it's there somewhere.

And I'd just like to prove that the Buttonwoods can have just as much fun as the Bastables ever did. More, in fact. Really, just the ordinary good times we have can be pretty exciting when we do them together. If you go now, you'll have a nice long afternoon to find that treasure."

They were still brimming over with questions, but Mom shooed them off. "Now go before you wake Small Sue," she said. "Or you'll have to stay and take care of her instead!"

They scampered off in a hurry. Treasure hunting sounded much more exciting than rocking Susie, any day!

"I wonder what Mom was talking about," Pudge said as they trotted down the lane. "Dad didn't put it there and neither did she."

"Maybe the twins did—before they went to Granddad's," Flora said. She scrambled through the bars after Betsy. "Ouch! That stupid thistle!"

"Here—I'll pull it out for you." Pudge took his big red hanky and, using it to shield his hand pulled the thistle away from Flora's bare foot. "That just goes to show you ought to wear shoes when you go hunting for treasure!"

"Hey, Pudge—the heifers are over there. Let's count 'em to make sure they're all here." Betsy walked over and began to count the brown heads. "Ten—eleven—twelve. There's one missing."

Pudge looked thoughtful. Then he counted again. "You're right, Betsy. Maybe we'd better try walking the fence while

we look for treasure. Then we can see whether one of them broke out."

They plunged into the woods along a cow trail that wound in and out past fallen logs and over roots and rocks. Now and then, there were blackberry briers higher than their heads.

"Ouch! Take it easy," Flora complained, as one brier slapped her in the face while another caught at her curls.

"You have to expect some hardships when you go treasure hunting," Pudge pointed out. But he did slow up. "If we cut across here, there ought to be a better trail right along the line fence—"

They broke through to it a minute later—an old trail, with branches thick above their heads and moss and leaves like a carpet under their feet. It was so quiet that they lowered their voices when they talked, without realizing that they did it.

Suddenly, a grouse flew up with a whir of wings right under Betsy's nose. She gave a shriek and a little jump, because she was so surprised. They all stopped to stare.

"Why, Pudge! She's hurt," Betsy said, as the grouse circled back again, and then ran just ahead of them, dragging her wing.

"Oh, no, she isn't. She's just trying to fool us," Pudge said. "Her babies are around here somewhere—look close. They look just like little brown leaves."

"There!" Flora said, pointing. "See! There's one of them."

And sure enough, they all spied a baby grouse sitting perfectly still and trying to look as if it weren't alive at all. Flora sneaked up softly, softly—closer and closer. Then, just as she put out her hand, the tiny thing gave a sharp peep and ran forward. The mother grouse circled back again, flew almost in Flora's face, and then disappeared.

"Well! Do you suppose that was Mom's treasure?" Betsy asked as they started on.

"I don't think so," Pudge said, "How could she know they were back here, anyway?"

"Anyway, it's adventure number one for us," Flora said. "The baby grouse would have been a nice present for Peter, but I'm glad it's safe with its mother, after all."

The others agreed with her. They walked on along the line fence trail, while Pudge checked the fence as they went.

"Not a break big enough for a cow, so far," he said. "I wonder where Brindle got to. Say—I'm getting hot. There's a spring down here somewhere. I've been back here with Dad, so I know. But I'm not sure just where—"

At that minute, Flora, who was forging off the trail into the ferns, slid down over the edge of a bank and sat down hard.

"I think I've found your spring, Pudge," she said. "Anyway, it feels wet in here."

"Well, don't keep sitting in it like that." Betsy said. "You'll have the water all muddy and we'll never be able to drink it."

"Well, I like that!" Flora sounded indignant. "Nobody asks

me whether I broke a leg or skinned my knee or anything like that. Oh, no! They're just afraid I'm muddying the water. Of course, I like sitting down in an ice-cold spring, like this, Betsy. I do it all the time—for fun."

She stood up and glared at the others. For a minute, they glared right back. Then Pudge and Betsy burst out laughing —they just couldn't help it. Flo did look so funny, standing there all dripping wet with her face like a thundercloud.

"Don't be mad, Flo dear," Betsy said, as soon as she could talk. "If you could see yourself, you'd laugh too. Honest, you would. You look exactly like that old rooster after his tumble into the horse trough—remember?"

"I suppose I do look funny," Flora admitted. She grinned, too. "Anyway, the spring is a little higher up—see the water coming out from under those rocks? So I didn't really sit down in it. It's nice and clear. And there's even an old tin cup.

They all drank and drank, because the water was so refreshing and cold. Then they started on along the trail, with Pudge walking close to the fence while the girls kept in the open. Finally, they turned a corner and headed back uphill again, right through the underbrush.

"That's where our place joins Broadwater's," Pudge explained. "This will be the home stretch now—it seems as if we were miles and miles from anywhere, but before too long, we'll be coming out right back of the sugar camp—"

At that minute, as they crashed through the bushes, a brown face appeared at Betsy's elbow, while a gruff voice said "Moo —oo—oo!" almost in her ear. It was so close and so unexpected that she stopped where she was. Flora and Pudge both plowed right into her.

"What is it?" Flora gasped.

For a second, Betsy couldn't speak. Then she parted the bushes beside her and said, "Why, it's Brindle! Here she is, Pudge. And she has a little black-and-white calf with her, too."

The calf was standing on unsteady little legs, while Brindle stood nearby. When Pudge moved to touch its knobby little head, she moved uneasily.

"We'd better not bother her. It's her first and she's nervous," Pudge said. "I'll tell Dad it's here, then he can help me bring them both home this evening."

With a last little pat on the soft little coat, they turned away and trudged on home. In a few minutes, they left the woods behind and walked past the sugar camp up to the barn.

"You know," Pudge said, "I guess Mom was right, at that."

"What do you mean?" Betsy demanded. "The calf was the treasure she meant, of course. Dad knew Brindle had a calf back there somewhere and wanted us to find it for him."

"Yes, I know—that was the treasure. But she said something else too—don't you remember?"

"I know," Flora said suddenly. " 'Just the ordinary good

times we have can be pretty exciting when we do them together.' Isn't that what you mean, Pudge?"

Pudge nodded his head. "That's it. And I agree. As far as
I'm concerned, those Bastable children don't have a thing
on us!"

And Betsy and Flora agreed with him, although they were
too out of breath to say a word.

Chapter 8

Curiosity Killed a Mouse

Peter stood beside the kitchen stove, waiting for the other Buttonwoods to get ready for a hike up Meadow Mountain.

"Do we have everything we need?" Betsy asked. A little frown creased her forehead as she counted, "Three gunny sacks for nuts, the lunch basket, a tin can to drink out of—"

"I have an extra little bag in case I find something to add to my collection," Pudge added.

The rest (even Mom) all groaned. That collection of Pudge's had overflowed the playhouse by now and spread all over the house again, with speckled rocks scattered through bureau drawers among the sheets, pressed leaves in every book in the house, and odds and ends showing up in the

66

queerest places (like the bluebird feather Mom found in a gravy boat).

"I'd take it easy with stuff like that for a while, Pudge," Mom advised. "The Buttonwoods will have to move to the barn if this keeps up much longer."

"I won't bring anything that isn't really important," Pudge promised with a grin.

Peter put his hand deep into his pocket, where Midget Mouse was lurking right then. He liked to collect things, too, but he didn't care about dead stuff. He wanted something alive, like Midget. Something you could keep in your pocket, that felt warm and soft—something that was always there, so if you got scared or felt unhappy, it could comfort you.

"The kind of things I collect aren't all over the place all the time," he said.

Then he wished he hadn't spoken, because everybody looked at him.

"You'd better not take Midget this time, Pete," Pudge said. "We don't feel like hunting over the whole of Meadow Mountain for that disappearing mouse of yours."

"I'll say," Flora added. "At least Pudge's collection stays more or less put. We don't have to go chasing it all over creation."

"I'll be careful," Peter promised. "Midget won't get out of my pocket this time. You'll see."

He put his hand into his pocket again. The rest just didn't

understand how important Midget was—they didn't know that feeling him, there in his pocket, made Peter feel brave about being alone and kept him from crying when he hurt himself. And if he ever needed something like that, it would be while he was scrambling around on Meadow Mountain, getting his arms scratched by briers and his knees skinned up on the rocks.

"Now just a minute," Mom said. "Let's think about this, Peter. You know it wouldn't be fair to spoil the whole trip for everybody else, don't you?"

Peter nodded his head. He looked glum because he thought he knew what was coming next, but Mom surprised him.

"You can take Midget, if you want to," she said. "Just re- member—if he escapes, he's gone. You won't be able to catch him again; so don't insist on trying. And you're not to whine or complain about it, either."

"Oh, sure—sure, Mom." Peter would have agreed to any- thing, he was so happy.

Dad Buttonwood walked into the kitchen just then. "Why don't you youngsters get started before the squirrels gather every hickory nut on Meadow Mountain?" he demanded. "The weather is perfect—clear and blue, with a few leaves drifting down already. You've got a whole wonderful Satur- day ahead of you; so don't waste it in chatter here in the kitchen."

He stood in the kitchen doorway, waving as the Button-

wood children started off. Mom and Small Sue stood just behind him, watching them go.

They were a queer-looking crowd, loaded down with gunny
sacks and baskets, but they turned off the road and took a
trail up the mountain before too long, and so it didn't really
matter.

"I hope we get every one of these sacks full of hickory nuts,"
Crish said.

"We couldn't lug them home if they were really full,"
Betsy reminded her.

"And on a day like this, a hike will be tops even if we don't
see a nut anywhere," Pudge said, looking up at the blue sky,
then down at the golden leaves he was shuffling with his feet.

It was a super day—they all agreed to that. And they did
find a lot of hickory nuts, too, gathering them from under the
indignant noses of chattering squirrels (who felt that the
Buttonwoods had no right to take their property).

After scrambling around a bit, the children discovered a
spring, where they drank their fill of ice-cold water. Then,
sitting on moss-covered logs, they ate the lunch Mom had
packed, right down to the last crumb.

"Now we can use this basket for nuts, too," Betsy said,
pointing to the empty lunch basket. "Peter can carry that."

Peter put his hand into his pocket and let Midget nibble his
finger. "Okay," he agreed.

"Crish could carry that little sack Pudge brought," Flora

said with a giggle. "He hasn't found a thing for his collection so far."

"I've been too busy to look," Pudge explained. "From now on, I'm going to really keep my eyes open. With all this big mountain, there's bound to be something—"

And, sure enough, it wasn't long till they came to a place where the mountain leveled off a little into a kind of clearing. There, on a tree, hung a big gray hornets' nest.

"Oh, boy! Just what I've wanted for ages," Pudge said.

"But, Pudge," Betsy protested, "are you sure the hornets aren't—well, at home right now?"

"You know what Mom would say if she were here," Peter told him. Then as the others stared, he added, " 'Curiosity killed a cat,' you know."

"Well, it will take more than a few hornets to kill me," Pudge said. "I'm going to find out what's what, anyway."

He sent several pebbles glancing against the side of the nest and nothing happened. Then he walked over toward the tree, with the others trailing after. They all dropped their bags of nuts as Pudge shinned up the trunk and inched his way along the limb. It wasn't till he was twisting the branch that the nest was on that they heard it—an angry buzzing, followed by a stream of hornets, ready to fight for their lives.

Pudge dropped down and raced across the clearing, with the rest after him as fast as they could go.

"Whew! That was close," he admitted, as he dropped down

among the ferns to rest himself. "I suppose we might as well give up and go home, as far as that nest is concerned. I don't have anything here to smoke them out, anyway."

"But our hickory nuts, Pudge!" Flora wailed. "They're all out there, under that tree."

Pudge rolled over and groaned. "What goops we were to take them with us! Well, I'm not going home without them, that's sure. Not if I have to sit here till those hornets go to bed!"

"Oh, Pudge! We couldn't find our way home after dark," Betsy protested. "Besides, think how worried Mom and Dad would be by then!"

"Okay—okay," Pudge said. "But at least we can wait a little while. Maybe they'll calm down enough so that we can risk going back."

He began to shuffle around in the ferns with one hand, "Hey—look here, Peter! See what I found!"

They all looked, of course. Pudge was holding a little plug from a knothole in his hand, and it was shaped exactly like a mouse, crouched down, ready for a nap.

"Why, it's Midget!" Crish said.

Peter's hand went into his pocket right away. "No, it isn't," he began. Then his face changed. They all knew, even before Peter began to howl, that Midget was gone.

In spite of what Mom had said, they did hunt for a little while. But they knew it was hopeless from the first. Why, they weren't even sure just where on Meadow Mountain Midget had dropped out of Peter's pocket.

"I'll tell you what, Pete," Pudge said as they all settled down to rest for a minute. "Here's this knothole that looks like Midget—well, I'll carve a little mouse for you out of it."

"And this one won't ever run away," Betsy added gently.

Peter looked at them all. They were being swell about it, but Midget was gone. "It won't be the same," he said. "Midget was furry and warm."

Then he straightened up. "But it will be better than nothing," he added.

"Good for you, Pete!" Pudge said.

By the time the wooden Midget was finished, with a smooth head and neat little ears, the hornets seemed to have settled down again. The Buttonwoods all sneaked out into the clearing together, grabbed their sacks of nuts, then ran pell-mell down the mountain. Before long they were back in their own kitchen, telling Mom all about it.

She put her arm around Peter when she heard about Midget. "We all have to learn to face up to the things we decide for ourselves," she said. "It's part of growing up, but sometimes it is hard. I hope Peter didn't ruin your hike."

"He didn't!"

"Oh, Mom—he was just swell about it!"

"Just as good as he could be—he cried only a little bit, right at first."

"Now let's not all talk at once," but Mom smiled as she said that. Then she turned to Peter with a special smile, just for him. It made him feel warm and happy inside.

Midget was gone for good, Peter knew. And the little wooden mouse in his pocket could never quite take his place, of course. But it was pleasant to think of him racing around on the mountain perhaps finding a family for himself out there. Besides, now that Peter was growing up so fast, he didn't really need a little mouse in his pocket to help him feel big and brave.

"Anyway, we were all wrong about one thing," Crish said suddenly.

"What was that?" Mom asked.

"When Pudge wanted to look at that hornets' nest, we told him curiosity killed a cat," she explained. "But this time it didn't."

For a minute they all looked at Peter to see how he was taking it. But Peter grinned right back at them.

"Sure—I know," he said. "This time curiosity killed a mouse, and it was Midget!"

Chapter 9

Bookworm Betsy

The minute Betsy Buttonwood woke up that morning she knew something pleasant was going to happen. She lay there, feeling good without knowing just why—then she remembered. It was the first Friday of the month—bookmobile day at school! That meant she could choose three new books to read.

Betsy hopped out of bed in a hurry. She dressed and ran downstairs without waking Flora or Crish. Mom looked up in surprise when Betsy came into the big kitchen, just as she was starting fire in the range.

"You're up early this morning," she said.

"It's bookmobile day. And I forgot to put last month's books in my schoolbag. If I forget to take those back, I can't get any others today." Betsy shuddered at the thought, and whisked the books from the clock shelf right away.

Mom looked sober. "You won't be any good to anybody for a week or so again, I suppose. You're such a good helper, Betsy, until you get your nose into a book."

"I don't mean to forget things, Mom. Honest I don't. But I get so interested in reading that I can't help it." Betsy felt guilty, remembering how often Mom had to remind her to do her work when she was reading.

The other children came piling down the back stairs then, and Small Susie cried from her crib. After that, there wasn't a minute's time to think of anything except getting ready for school. At the Buttonwood house, on school mornings, everybody had to fly around, with so many getting ready all at the same time. With five of them going to school—well, that meant a lot of hankies and buttons, pigtails and lunches, to see to. But today, Betsy didn't mind. She wouldn't mind anything on bookmobile day!

That evening she came home with the three books she had chosen.

"I thought I'd get another Bobbsy Twin book, but Miss Temple doesn't think I should read so many of them," she told Mom. "She talked quite a lot about which books are good and which aren't. And she said it's all right to read some that aren't such good writing, but if we read too many, they'll spoil our appetites for the really good ones."

6

"Good for Miss Temple," Mom said. "And what else did she have to say?"

"She says we can learn things from good books. All kinds of things—like how to get along with other people, and understanding people who live in different countries, and finding out about nature and the things around us."

Mom looked up from the hem she was putting in a dress that had once belonged to Flora (and before that, to Betsy), which was now being shortened for Crish.

"That depends partly on the person who is reading, too, Betsy. You should read, of course—especially good books. But you won't really learn much if you keep your nose in a book all the time. For instance, you won't learn to make friends if you say, 'Go away. I'm reading,' every time the other children come around. You have to take time out to live what you learn, too."

"I suppose so," Betsy said slowly. "Anyway, I got three new books: *Little Women, Hans Brinker,* and *Five Little Peppers and How They Grew.* See, Mom?"

Mom took the stack of books and leafed through them. "What memories they bring back!" she said.

Betsy looked surprised. "Did you ever read these, Mom?"

"Every one," Mom told her with a chuckle. "Oh, I used to be a bookworm too, Betsy. Leave *Little Women* here if you don't mind. I'd like to browse through it a little if I get time."

Just then the twins burst into the kitchen.

"Grandpa's here," Crish sang out.

"And he wants some of us to come for the weekend!" Peter added.

"And it's our turn to go!" Crish clapped her hands.

Flora appeared out of thin air at the first word. "Mine, too," she said. "I was sick when Pudge and Betsy went last time."

"That's right." Mom got up and folded her sewing. "I'd better help you get your things together."

"I don't want to go," Betsy said quickly. She patted the cover of *Five Little Peppers* with one hand.

"I'd rather go to Grandpa's than read, any day," Flora said bluntly.

It did seem quiet around the house after the twins and Flora were gone, but Betsy was rather glad. After supper, she settled down to her book and read all evening. The only answers Pudge got out of her were "What?" and "Is that so?" And Mom had to remind her three times before she finally got off to bed.

Next morning, right after breakfast, Betsy slipped upstairs. She squatted down on her bed and opened *Five Little Peppers*.

"Mom will call me to do the dishes in about two minutes, but I can read a page or so before then," she said to herself.

Then she started reading and forgot everything else. She forgot the bread dough Mom had mixed that morning and asked her to watch. She forgot that Mom was left alone with the dishes and Small Sue, who was fussy because of colic. She forgot the kitchen floor she was supposed to scrub and the lamps that needed cleaning and filling. When Betsy read, she read. Nothing else had a chance in her mind.

Later—what seemed like a long, long time later—Betsy looked up with a sigh. She felt the way she always did when she finished a book—half glad she was done and half sorry there wasn't more to read. She moved, then winced. Her leg prickled from sitting on it so long. And the back of her neck was stiff from bending over.

"Seems awfully late. I'd better hike down and help Mom," Betsy thought. She jumped up, feeling guilty. " 'Sfunny she didn't call me before this."

Betsy ran down the back stairs to the kitchen. "Oh, Mom," she began. Then she stood there and stared. The dishes were still on the table just as the Buttonwoods had left them when they got up from breakfast. Leftover oatmeal had turned to a queer brown-coated lump. Bits of egg made a design on the plates. And the milk in its pitcher had a lumpy look.

Betsy glanced at the clock. Eleven o'clock! And no sign of dinner on the stove. The bread dough Mom had fixed that morning was half out of its pan, dangling over the edge of the kitchen stool.

"Where is Mom?" Betsy said as she pushed the bread back with one hasty punch. She hardly knew she'd said it aloud until Mom answered from the dining room.

"I'm in here."

Betsy went in. Mom was lying on the sofa with two pillows behind her back and a glass of water on the floor besides her. She was reading *Little Women.*

"Are you sick?" Betsy couldn't help asking that. It seemed so strange to see Mom lying there, in broad daylight, just reading.

"No, Betsy. I'm just tired," Mom said. "I've been rereading *Little Women.*"

"But—but it's time to get dinner."

"Is it?" Mom turned back to her book in an unconcerned way that gave Betsy a queer cold feeling in the pit of her stomach. "You can get something for Dad and Pudge, can't you?"

Betsy went back to the kitchen. "She must be sick and just doesn't want to worry me," she thought. "Oh, dear—the fire's out. What in this world can I have for dinner that won't take long? I know—pancakes and sausage. But I'll have to hurry."

Betsy did fly around then. Between frying pancakes, she scraped the breakfast dishes and set them in the sink. By then the bread was creeping out of bounds again.

"Oh, dear!" Betsy sighed. "As sure as sure, if I start on the bread, I'll forget and burn the pancakes. I wonder if it would hurt to just knead it down once more and leave it till later. I guess—"

At that minute Small Sue woke up from her nap. Betsy

could hear her sleepy gurgle, but (between the pancakes and
bread) she simply didn't have time for her. Susie's gurgle
changed to a lusty yell. By the time Betsy finally went for
her, she was red in the face and very cross.

"Now be a good girl while Betsy gets dinner." Betsy said
as she plumped Small Sue into her high chair and gave her
a rattle to play with.

But Small Susie's feelings had been deeply hurt. She didn't
want a rattle—she didn't want to be in her high chair—she
wasn't having any of that "good girl" talk. Before Betsy made
it back to her pancakes, she had pushed the rattle to the floor
and begun to cry again.

Betsy had a hectic time after that, but she finally did get
dinner on the table. Luckily, Pudge and Dad Buttonwood
were a little late coming in. Mom came out to eat, but she
went back to her book right afterward.

First thing after dinner, Betsy kneaded the bread dough and
formed it into loaves. Then she tackled the dishes. And what
a job that was! Small Sue started fussing again, and so Betsy
stopped long enough to give her a bottle and tuck her into
her crib. When the dishes were done, she brought potatoes
from the cellar and put them on to boil for potato salad next
day. Then she scrubbed the kitchen floor. After that, she
cleaned and filled the lamps.

Late that afternoon, Betsy sat down beside the table and
with one elbow on the clean oilcloth, held her head in her

hands. Four o'clock already! And my, but she was tired!

"Tired, dear?" Mom asked from the doorway behind her.

"A little. Feeling better, Mom?"

"Wonderful!" Mom said. "I haven't felt so rested for weeks. Your bread smells good. Let's have some of it with butter and honey. And some hot chocolate, too."

"I'll get it," Betsy said, half getting up.

"Sit still." Mom pushed Betsy down again. "You deserve a rest—you've worked so hard. By the way—did you enjoy your book, Betsy?"

"Oh, it was super, Mom! The fun those youngsters had, poor as they were. But I liked it much better before they left the Little Brown House than afterward."

Mom stirred chocolate syrup into some milk and set it on the range. Then she began to slice the bread. "Polly Pepper was such a help to her mother—just the way you are to me," she said.

"Oh, Mom!" was all Betsy could say.

"Well, you really are—most of the time. It's only when you get buried in a book that you forget."

"I know," Betsy said slowly. "Then you have to do my work."

Mom's eyes twinkled. "Not this time, I didn't."

Betsy stared at her. "Did you do it on purpose?" she asked.

" 'What's sauce for the goose is sauce for the gander,' " Mom said. "I got the idea out of *Little Women*. Marmee did that to her four girls when they decided loafing would be more fun than doing their share of the work. She just walked off and let them see how they got along. I couldn't do that—so I just read."

Mom pushed Betsy's slice of bread across the table to her. "I wanted to help you understand what I said yesterday—that how much you get out of a book depends a great deal on you. That's true of any book—even the Bible. You were reading about a girl who helped her mother, but it didn't make you see that I needed help. Quite the contrary! I wanted you to see that for yourself."

"I do see it," Betsy said. She took a huge bite of bread and honey. "And I know now exactly how you feel when I sit in a corner and leave all the work for you. If I ever do it again, you can just whisper *Little Women* to me, and I'll stop in a hurry."

"Good!" Mom smiled at Betsy. "Now I'm rested and ready for work. You run along and relax till suppertime."

Betsy gulped down the last of her cocoa and stood up. "Oh, thank you, Mom! And if you're finished with *Little Women*, I guess I'll start it. I'd like to read that chapter for myself!"

Chapter 10

Buttonwood Scrapbook

Betsy Buttonwood stood at the range, stirring a kettle of corn meal mush. Her glance went around the big kitchen, from the twins huddled on the wood box, past Pudge hunched over the table, to Flora crouched in Mom's rocker with her feet pulled up under her. It was the same kitchen, of course—but it didn't seem the same, somehow. It even felt different—

"How long do you s'ppose Mom will have to stay at the hospital?" Peter asked solemnly.

"Maybe Dad'll tell us that when he gets home," Betsy said briskly. She glanced up at the clock, tick-tocking to itself on the shelf over the table. "Visiting hours last till eight; so he should be here by half past or a little after."

Crish leaned forward so far she almost tumbled off the wood box. "How about Small Sue?" she demanded. "She'll be lonesome at Aunt Erma's without any of us there. I know she will. She'd be better off here—"

Pudge looked up from the scrapbook of pressed leaves he was making. "Cut it out, Crish," he said. His voice was gruff, but he didn't sound angry. "Dad explained all that to us— remember? What would we do with Susie during the day— take her to school with us?"

"Miss Temple would love that," Flora put in. She tried to smile but couldn't quite make it.

"We're all (Pudge and Flo and I) pretending to be cheerful because of the twins," Betsy thought to herself. "But underneath we feel just as scared and lost as they do."

Flora scrambled to her feet. "Why don't we make popcorn?" she said. "And hot cocoa would taste good, too. That way we could have it all ready for Dad when he comes. I know he'll be half frozen."

The Buttonwoods got busy in a hurry. Betsy pulled her kettle of mush to the back of the stove where its slow plop! plop! couldn't bother anybody. Flora helped Crish make cocoa (with unusual patience) while Pudge actually let Peter pop the corn in the big Dutch oven by himself, with only a little help in lifting it off when it was finished.

Betsy sat on Mom's rocker, rocking and thinking. "This is all right for one evening," she thought. "But what if Mom has to stay in the hospital for a week or so? We can't make pop-corn and cocoa every evening, just to keep the twins happy. Oh, dear, they're a worse problem than Small Sue would have been."

She let her gaze wander around until she caught sight of Pudge's scrapbook on the table. He had pasted a pressed tree leaf on each page. Below it, he wrote in all kinds of infor-mation about the tree itself. Even as Betsy looked, a sudden idea popped into her mind. But before she had a chance to share it with the rest, the door behind her opened and Dad Buttonwood walked in.

"Well, well—this looks cozy!" he said. "Whew, but it's cold outside."

Crish and Peter threw themselves on him.

"There's popcorn—lots of it," Peter said. "I did the popping all by myself."

"And I made the cocoa. Flora helped me only a tiny bit," Crish put in.

Over their heads, Dad gave the three oldest Buttonwoods an approving look. Later on, after the twins were in bed, he talked to them about it.

"Dr. Albright says Mom's going to be in the hospital a week at least," he told them. "Aunt Erma will do the wash-ing; so I know we can manage the rest of the work. But keep-ing the twins happy is something else again. We're going to have to work together on that—the way you did this evening."

"I have an idea," Betsy said eagerly. She gave the mush in the kettle one last stir, then began to ladle it out into pans to cool. "Why don't we make a scrapbook—all about our own family?"

Pudge and Flora and Dad looked bewildered.

"I don't see—" Flora began.

"Each page of the scrapbook would be about something that really happened to us," Betsy explained. "We'd decide for ourselves whether we'd want to write it up like a story or draw little pictures about it or paste in some souvenirs—or maybe use a little of all three."

Light dawned in Pudge's face. "That sounds super to me!"

"We could do a page on Small Sue—when she was born last spring," Flora said. "We have a picture of her we could use."

"I think it's a good idea, Betsy," Dad said. "It will work— if you all pitch in and act as if you were having fun, too."

"We're going to," Betsy said firmly.

It was hard to live up to that the next evening, though. After school there was lots of work to be done and everything seemed so awkward without Mom on hand to help and advise. After supper, Betsy didn't really want to do a thing in the world except settle down in Mom's rocker and read. She had to make a real effort to get the twins started on the Buttonwood scrapbook instead.

"I'm going to do a page about Hooty, the Owl," Crish announced as soon as she heard about the scrapbook.

"I'll tell about our treasure hunt," Pudge said with a grin. "When we found Brindle's calf, you know."

Peter sat up straight. "Lets see—I guess I'll put in something about Midget. I could draw a mouse, just as easy. And I can use my wooden mouse to look at, while I do it."

"What'll you have, Betsy?" Flora asked.

"Oh, I haven't decided—yet," she said. "I'll help the twins with theirs till I think of something."

After that, Betsy was too busy mixing up paste (from flour and water), hunting for the scissors, supplying magazine pictures to cut out, fixing brown wrapping paper pages, and giving hints to all the rest to notice how the time was flying. Dad was back from the hospital before the Buttonwoods knew it.

Next evening, the rest worked at their scrapbook pages again. They were all (even the three oldest Buttonwoods) beginning to be really interested. Dad had picked up the washing at Aunt Erma's; so Betsy ironed all evening—when she wasn't telling Peter that his picture of Midget was super or explaining to Crish that you were apt to start going uphill with your writing when you didn't have any lines on your paper, but it didn't really matter a bit.

"You haven't started on your page yet, Betsy," Pudge said, when she finally slid the ironing board into its place in the pantry.

"I know. I'll get at it one of these days. I have so much to see to here at home since Mom's not here."

"I'm going to make another page—about Mom going to the hospital," Crish said. "This one's all finished—see?"

While they were admiring Crish's handwork, Dad walked in, back from seeing Mom. After he had reported that she was getting along just fine, he said, "I've been telling her about this scrapbook you're making and she says she'd like to see it, too."

They all looked at each other. "Why didn't we think of that before?" Pudge said. "Aren't we goops, though?"

"We could send her the pages that are finished already, then add later ones as we make them," Flora suggested.

Betsy didn't say anything. It was a good idea, but she hadn't had time to make any page herself. Of course, Mom would understand that she'd been too busy, but it would have been nice to have something to send to her, too.

The next day, Betsy saw Pudge and Flora whispering together at school. After a bit, they cornered the twins and discussed something with them. Betsy did wonder what it was all about, but just then the bell rang and she forgot all about it. But as soon as they got home from school that evening, she knew!

"Say, Betsy, I'm going to help Pudge with the chickens tonight," Crish announced.

"And I'm going to carry the wood in, all by myself," Peter added.

"That way, Flo won't have a thing to do except get supper," Pudge said with a grin.

"But—but that's my job!" Betsy looked puzzled. She couldn't understand it.

"Not this evening, it isn't," Flora said firmly. "This evening, your job is to finish a page of the Buttonwood scrapbook before it's time for Dad to go to the hospital to see Mom. Now, scat! Go up to the back bedroom, where it's warm, and work as fast as you can. And don't worry about a thing."

Sitting beside the kitchen stove pipe in the back bedroom, Betsy felt suddenly warm and happy. It was terrible having Mom in the hospital, but it was pretty good to belong to a family like the Buttonwoods, too. She thought about their kitchen and the good feeling it always had—the feeling you get when you're with people you like.

"I know what I'm going to put on my page," she decided. "I'm going to call it 'The Buttonwood family works together,' and I'll use little drawings about each of us, doing something for the rest. I'll label them so Mom can't miss it."

Just as Betsy dotted the last "i," Dad popped his head in at the door. "What goes on here? The famous scrapbook?"

"Oh, yes!" Betsy waved her page in front of his eyes. "Mine is about the things we do for each other. Like it?"

Dad looked and looked. He laughed at the little sketches. Pudge was hoeing in the garden, while Peter carried in wood. Crish rocked Small Sue in Mom's big rocker. Dad brought in a big armful of groceries. Flora dusted the living room, and Betsy herself was baking bread.

7

There were a lot of sketches of Mom, too. She was washing clothes, ironing, mending, cleaning.

"What's this one, here in the corner?" Dad asked.

"Oh, I forgot to label it!" Betsy said. "Can't you guess what it is, Dad?"

Dad looked at the row of little stick figures Betsy had drawn. A very tiny stick figure squatted at one end of the line, and the tallest of all was at the other end. Six others, of various sizes, straggled in between.

"I'd guess this is the Buttonwoods, all in a row. But I can't decide what we're doing. Just holding out our hands in front of us, perhaps?"

"It's supposed to represent one of Mom's little sayings," Betsy said with a giggle.

Then she took her pencil and printed "Many hands make light work" under the picture.

"Yoo-hoo-hoo!" Flora called from downstairs. "Dad, you were supposed to tell Betsy that supper's ready."

"That's right—so I was!" Dad looked at Betsy and grinned. "And I've suddenly remembered that I'm hungry as a bear. Let's go eat."

Dad took their scrapbook pages along to the hospital that evening. And after that, they all made as many pages as they could and sent them with Dad each time he went.

Then came the big day—when Dad brought Mom home from the hospital. She hugged them all by turns. And they all hugged Small Sue, who jumped and crowed like a little cricket.

"I did enjoy that scrapbook of yours," Mom said. "I liked it all. When I saw Betsy's page, I could lie there and look at it— and think of you all, helping each other. I think knowing that helped me get well faster."

Betsy looked around the big kitchen. They had worked hard, of course.

"But it wasn't so bad, really, Mom," she said.

"Because we all worked together," Flora added.

Then with a wink at the others, Pudge said, " 'Many hands make light work,' you know."

Mom laughed with the others. She didn't mind because she knew they had really learned how true that saying was.

Chapter 11

Prize for Pudge

Pudge, Betsy, and Flora Buttonwood, just home from school, burst into the big kitchen. They were starved and bubbling over with news.

"Guess what, Mom?" Pudge slammed his books on the table, just missing a loaf of freshly baked bread by an inch. The oil lamps on the shelf above clattered. "Yum—that bread smells super!"

"We're having a Hobby Day at school," Betsy put in as she pulled off her hood and hung it on its hook behind the door.

Flora looked up from her usual battle-with-the-rubbers. "It's a contest—anybody in the whole school can enter it, Miss Temple says."

94

"*May* enter it, you mean," Mom said. She got up to look at the bread still in the oven, then sat down to her mending again. Sometimes it seemed to the children that Mom was mending all the time. But with six of them—no wonder! "So that's what Crish and Peter were trying to tell me."

"Those twins! They always get to tell everything first," Pudge complained. "Miss Temple shouldn't let them come home before the rest of us do, that's what!"

Mom settled herself comfortably. "They knew so little and talked so fast that I couldn't figure out what they were trying to say," she said. "So you go right ahead as if it were all news to me."

Pudge planted himself right in front of Mom, his forgotten rubbers leaving a puddle under each foot. "It's like this—Miss Temple says anybody who has a collection of any kind may bring it to school for Hobby Day. We're to fix them up real neat, you know. Then our parents can come to see them. And there will be all kinds of prizes. And a grand prize for the best collection in the whole school—whew!" Pudge whistled through his teeth.

"It's the most bea-yu-ti-ful book in the world," Flora broke in. "*A Nature Atlas* with pictures of fish and trees and butterflies and—oh, just everything."

"I'm starved," Betsy announced loudly. She slipped the bread knife from the rack. "How about a slice of fresh bread, Mom?"

"Me, too," Pudge said, forgetting Hobby Day for a minute. "With butter and honey."

"Not so fast now!" Mom dropped the sock she was darning and took the knife herself. "I'll cut you each one piece—and no more. I know exactly how that loaf will look by the time you three finish hacking away at it!"

For a while the big kitchen was filled with a sticky kind of silence, while the bread-and-butter-and-honey disappeared. Then Pudge started in again.

"I have my eye on that grand prize," he said. "That book is really something. Why, you could identify practically anything you'd find in it."

"Nick Satterlie claims he's going to win it," Betsy said.

Pudge frowned until his freckles all ran together across his forehead. "Oh—Nick! He's always talking. Just because that sailor uncle of his sends him shells from all over the world for his collection, he thinks he can beat all the rest of us. He's just a big show-off, that's all."

"Don't talk like that, Pudge," Mom said.

"But he is terrible, Mom!" Pudge protested.

"Nobody at school likes him—really!" Betsy added. "He brags like anything."

"Oh, I believe you," Mom said quietly. "I suppose Nick does show off and brag. But just remember that he doesn't have any mother, either."

They all did remember, then—standing there in the big cozy

kitchen. They thought of Nick's granny, who was forever complaining about her nerves and always hushed him up the minute he stepped inside the house. Of Nick's father, who was kind to him in his way, but terrible when he lost his temper. Most of all, they thought of Nick coming home from school to grab a bite to eat as quietly as he could, then race across the road to the store—with no mom to go to with smashed thumbs or heartaches.

"I do feel sorry for him, in a way," Pudge admitted. "But he is such a pill to have around, I can't keep it up for long."

"Just don't forget that you aren't perfect, either," Mom said. "Especially when you track mud all over my clean kitchen floor."

"I forgot about my rubbers—honest I did, Mom." Pudge took them off and began mopping up tracks. "But just the same, I'd like to have that grand prize. And I'm going to try for it, too."

"With what?" Flora demanded. "Your collection?"

Betsy and Flora both laughed, and even Mom's mouth twitched a little. Pudge didn't really mind—his collection was good for a laugh in the Buttonwood family at any time.

He'd started it years before with a bluebird feather, and from there it increased until it spilled all over the house. During the summer, he'd transferred it to the playhouse for a while, but lately it had overflowed even that. Pudge lugged home bits of lichen, rocks, wasps' nests, beetles, butterflies—

anything, everything. They fell out of closets on people's heads and cluttered up drawers.

"Laugh all you want to," Pudge said. "I'm going to enter my collection—at least, part of it. And I'm going to win that *Nature Atlas,* too."

Afterward, he didn't feel so sure. Bits of rock—empty cocoons—birds' nests—oak apples. It would take some doing to get those things into shape, that was sure. And it would have to be really good, Pudge knew, if he wanted to win over Nick Satterlie's shell collection.

Nick didn't really care too much about it, himself. But he'd started it when he was a little tyke and after that, his seafaring uncle kept sending him shells from every port in the world, it seemed. He had boxes full of them in his closet now. Pudge had nosed through them once. And he knew that his idea would have to be something super before he could hope to top that shell collection.

Pudge sneaked out to Dad's shop to think things over. The girls were already busy with their exhibits. Betsy was working on an old button string, while Flora was pasting her three hundred and thirty-nine pictures of horses into a scrapbook. Even the twins were working on a collection of pictures of pets, while Peter bemoaned himself loudly that he didn't have Midget Mouse for an exhibit!

By himself in the shop, Pudge settled down on a nail keg with his chin in his hand. He had to think of something—time was running out on him fast. Oh, for some really super-duper idea!

"Well, the Thinker himself!" Dad said from behind him. Pudge whirled around so suddenly that the nail keg upset. He and Dad both grabbed for it, bumping their heads sharply, while the keg rolled across the floor, spilling nails as it went. Dad winked at Pudge. "Guess what Mom would say on this occasion if she were here."

"I know! 'It's no use crying over spilled nails!' "

"And I agree. There's a much more sensible thing to do and that is, pick them up."

Dad pulled the keg upright and began to scoop up nails in his hands, sifting them carefully out of the shavings. With a sigh, Pudge knelt to help him.

"Why so sober, young man?" Dad asked.

"It's this Hobby Day business, Dad. It has me stumped, and that's a fact."

"Your collection is a little out of hand, isn't it?"

"I'll say!" Pudge admitted. "I've got too many things and not enough good ones. And I do want that prize, Dad. That *Nature Atlas* is really something. Besides, if Nick Satterlie wins it, he won't be fit to live with at all any more."

At the mention of Nick, Dad looked sober, too. "I know Nick is hard to take, Pudge. But did you ever think about it that maybe he needs to win? Are you sure he isn't bragging just because he feels left out of things? Everything is unpleasant at home and he feels shoved around there. So he comes to school and brags because he needs to feel important somewhere."

"But that isn't the way to make people like him!" Pudge protested.

"I know. And I'm glad that you see it, but Nick evidently doesn't. I know you get tired of his bragging, Pudge, but I wish you'd be kind anyway. I feel sorry for him—really, I do."

"Okay, I will," Pudge agreed finally, but he didn't really want to do it. He knew how hard it would be.

"And now I have an idea that I think will be just the thing for your Hobby Day exhibit," Dad went on. "You remember that aquarium we have in the attic, don't you?"

Pudge stared. He couldn't imagine what in the world the old aquarium could have to do with Hobby Day, but the longer Dad talked, the bigger his eyes got. Before Dad finished, Pudge was nodding his head like mad.

"Why, that's the very thing! Oh, I'm sure it will be the best thing there. Say—thanks a lot for helping me, Dad."

"Let's keep it a secret from the others, shall we?" Dad said with a chuckle. "They'll be bursting with curiosity for sure!"

In the days that followed, Pudge was the busiest Button-wood of them all. He bustled around all over the place, when he wasn't working behind closed doors in Dad's shop. First, he lugged the old aquarium down from the attic. After that, a steady stream of things disappeared into the shop.

"Two pails of sand—a basket of moss—and Mom's scouring powder," Betsy said with a giggle. "Are you planning to scour the moss or the sand, Pudge?"

"Just never you mind," Pudge said loftily. "Wait till you see it—then you'll know."

"Better not act too highhanded," Dad warned Pudge. "You'll need help in carting all that junk out there."

"Junk!" Pudge was indignant. "My collection is not junk. Besides, they'll be so glad to get rid of it, they won't mind helping."

At first, Betsy and Flora declared loudly that he could just keep his old secret—see if they were going to break their backs helping him! But in the end, the whole family pitched in, except Small Sue, of course. Even the twins worked like little squirrels, digging things out of the most unexpected corners.

"Here's that hummingbird nest Aunt Erma gave Pudge," Betsy said with a chuckle. "Imagine—it was up in the corner cupboard."

"I wanted it where it wouldn't get smashed," Pudge explained.

After that, he spent every spare minute working as hard as he could, but it wasn't until Hobby Day itself that he finally finished. Then he carried his entry into the house. The big kitchen was empty, but when he came clomping in, everybody came running. Then such a clamor as there was, with all of them talking at once!

Pudge had filled the bottom of the aquarium with sand, topped with moss. One hill sprouted a little forest made of ground pine. Opposite it, stood a bare shrub and between the two hills glistened a tiny lake made from a broken mirror. Arranged in this setting were the very best things from Pudge's collection—rocks, cowbird eggs, butterflies perched here and there, beetles of all sizes and colors. And in one crotch of the shrub tree nestled the hummingbird nest, with two tiny navy-bean eggs in it.

For a background, Pudge used a piece of cardboard. Here he glued a mud dauber's nest, some pressed flowers, a monarch butterfly and its empty chrysalis, and a few bright leaves. In one corner was a neat list of everything in the collection.

"Oh, Pudge!" was all Betsy could say.

"It's really super—you're sure to win the grand prize," Flora told him, while Crish and Peter kept crowding up with, "Let me see, too! Let me see, too!"

"It's perfect, Pudge dear," Mom said. She smiled in a pleased way and Pudge was satisfied.

Just then, Pudge looked up at the clock, tick-tocking away by itself on the clock shelf. "Say! I'm supposed to show up early to help Miss Temple with some last-minute stuff. And I haven't fed the chickens yet—"

"I'll do them, Pudge," Betsy offered quickly.

Mom nodded her head. "That's right; let Betsy. Now, you'd better get dressed and scamper over there right away, because time does go so fast. We'll bring your exhibit in the car with us."

When Pudge got to the school, on the run, Miss Temple was already there.

"You know, I just had a last-minute brain storm," she told Pudge. "There's a wide board in the woodshed that would make a beautiful shelf at the windows—just perfect for displays. But I've hunted and hunted and I can't find any nails big enough for a job like that. Why don't you dash over to Satterlie's store and get some for me?"

"Sure thing, Miss Temple," Pudge agreed.

"You'll have to hurry—remember," she told him. "There's not a second to lose now."

"I'll cut across Blakely's pasture, and save time that way. I only hope Mr. Satterlie isn't home for supper when I get there."

But that was exactly what happened. The battered "Out to Lunch" sign was on the door.

"Now I've either got to sit here till he comes back or go pry him loose from his supper," Pudge muttered to himself. He hesitated a little, then crossed over to the house opposite. At any other time, he would have waited rather than risk rousing Mr. Satterlie's touchy temper, but tonight he just couldn't.

Nick came to the door when Pudge knocked.

"Hey, Dad. You're wanted at the store," he called over one shoulder.

"Don't stand there holding the door open, Nick!" Granny called. "You should know by now that it gives me neuritis to sit in a draft like this. I've told you often enough, but you're so thoughtless—"

Nick grabbed his jacket and stepped outside, slamming the door much harder than he would have had to. Beyond it, Pudge could hear Granny's voice, complaining on and on.

"Let's go on over," Nick said. "Dad will be out in just a second."

"All set with your collection, Nick?" Pudge said. He was more curious than interested, really.

Nick shrugged his shoulders. "Aw, who cares about Hobby Day? I've got the best collection in school of course. But all that's just a lot of sissy stuff, anyway. I'm just not going to bother to enter at all."

For just a minute, Pudge felt rather relieved. Now he wouldn't have to worry. He was sure that Nick was the only person in the whole school who had any chance against him.

Then he remembered what Dad had said. "Maybe he needs to win—he feels shoved around at home." Thinking of what Nick's home was like gave Pudge a queer cold feeling in the pit of his stomach. Then Mr. Satterlie came out, looking black and mumbling something about never getting a chance to eat a meal in peace, and Pudge didn't have time for any more thinking.

Inside the store, Mr. Satterlie began to dig nails out of a

keg, clattering them into a box on the scales. Afterward,
Pudge never could have told exactly what did happen. Nick
had been dodging around, acting as if he owned the store.
Somehow or other, he must have dodged too close to his dad's
elbow. Suddenly, nails flew in every direction.

There was one minute of terrible silence, while Mr. Satterlie
turned purple. "I—I didn't mean to," Nick faltered.

"Get out of here—and stay out!" Mr. Satterlie roared. "Always underfoot—you've got no business over here anyway."

His roar changed to a steady rumble, because Nick had
already dodged out through the door. But Pudge had caught
a glint of tears on his cheeks. And he remembered the time
he had spilled nails in Dad's shop. Dad Buttonwood had
made a joke about it and helped pick them up. Pudge thought
of Granny's whining voice and compared it with the cheerful
way Mom always talked them out of their troubles.

And suddenly, he knew that Dad was right. Nick needed
to win. Maybe—just maybe, he could do something about it.
It felt a little like putting your head into a lion's mouth, but
Pudge did it, anyway.

He leaned across the counter and said, "Mr. Satterlie."

The bushy eyebrows went up. "Hey?"

"You know we're having a Hobby Day at school, don't
you?"

"Don't know as I do. Nick did chatter some about it, I
guess, but it never sank in very far."

Pudge took a deep breath. "Nick has that super collection of shells, you know. I'm quite sure he could win the grand prize."

Mr. Satterlie suddenly woke up. For the first time, he looked as if he was really listening. "You think so?"

"I'm almost sure," Pudge said. "He has such a lot of shells from all over the world. But—"

"But what?"

"He isn't going to enter them."

Mr. Satterlie frowned. "The little chump! Why not?"

Pudge took another breath. He hoped he wasn't getting Nick into more trouble, but he just had to go on now. "I—I think it's because he feels that you don't care whether he does or not. It isn't too late yet, Mr. Satterlie. I'm sure Nick would enter if you helped him a little."

The silence stretched on and on in the little store. Pudge didn't know what Mr. Satterlie was thinking. Was he sorry that he hadn't encouraged Nick more? Or was he just taking a deep breath in order to tell Pudge Buttonwood to go and mind his own business?

Actually, he didn't do either one. All he said was a gruff, "We'll see," as he handed Pudge the nails.

For the next hour, Pudge was too busy to think about Nick. He helped Miss Temple put up her shelf by the window. Then they rearranged some of the other exhibits on it, although they did save one end for additional items.

"Everything's in but your collection, Pudge," Miss Temple said.

"And Nick's shells," Pudge added.

"He told me he isn't going to enter. This is all sissy stuff. And although he knows he has the best collection in the whole school, he's not going to bother."

"Well, he may change his mind yet, Miss Temple. Anyway, I'll save a place right here. If he doesn't come with it by the time you start to award prizes, I can just shift a couple of things around to fill up this gap."

"All right," Miss Temple agreed. "Now I want you to stand back by the door as people come in, Pudge. If anybody else brings in a last-minute item, bring it right up here and put it among the rest. I'll be too busy saying 'hello' to parents to bother."

Before long, the room started filling up. The whole Buttonwood family came early, and Pudge carried his entry up front. It did look neat! He took a quick glance around. There wasn't another thing in the whole exhibit to compare with it, he knew.

"Pudge!" Miss Temple called, and he hurried back to his post.

This time it was Nick Satterlie and his father. Pudge's eyes really popped when he saw them. So Mr. Satterlie had been sorry that he'd yelled at Nick like that!

"Here's my collection," Nick said. "I'll help you arrange it."

As they walked up front, Nick went on in a low tone: "I
don't know what got into Dad all of a sudden. He closed the
store half an hour early and came tearing over to the house.
And he said that sure, I ought to enter my collection of shells.
Then we both worked like mad to fix it up, ready to bring.
And he didn't yell at me at all, except when I dropped the
hammer right on his toe—and that time, I didn't really blame
him!"

"It looks good, Nick," Pudge said.

And it really did, too. The smaller shells were fastened in a
big flat case, with a glass cover. They formed a big spiral
design in it. The big fellows he put down in front. Pudge
picked one up and felt how smooth it was in his hands. He
held it to his ear and heard the distant roar of the sea in it.
And just to think of all the faraway places that little shell had
visited while he, Pudge Buttonwood, had never been very far
from home!

After everybody had a chance to look at the displays, Miss
Temple rang her little bell, just the way she always did after
recess. The school children squeezed on the benches up front,
while their parents settled down at desks at the back, as best
they could. Pudge grinned at Dad, who was having a lot of
trouble with those long legs of his. Mom sat on a chair beside
him, with Susie on her lap.

"I've asked several members of the school board to help me
decide about prizes," Miss Temple explained. "Mr. Broad-

water and Mr. Blakely don't have any youngsters here; so it seemed fair to ask them to help out."

Then she went on to name prize after prize for each of the different grades. Finally, it came time for the grand prize. So far, neither Pudge nor Nick had won anything. Pudge leaned forward in his seat. He could feel himself getting hot. Suppose—just suppose, now that Mr. Satterlie had come, Nick wouldn't win. Wouldn't that be awful?

"And now we come to the grand prize," Miss Temple said. "First prize for the most unusual way of displaying a collection goes to Pudge Buttonwood for his little scene in the aquarium."

Pudge simply couldn't breathe. He had wanted that *Nature Atlas* so much, but now he felt as if he could never bear to look at it again. But Miss Temple was going on.

"Another first prize goes to Nick Satterlie for his complete collection of shells. It is by far the most detailed and extensive. He will get a *Nature Atlas*, too, if he wants one."

Pudge looked across at Nick. His face got red, clear down to his shirt collar, but he wasn't looking around in that biggity way that annoyed the other children so much. Instead, he was looking back at his father, as if he were the only person in the room who really mattered.

Afterward, when Pudge went up to Nick, he wasn't bragging either. The Buttonwoods talked about it on the way home.

"He always acts so—so show-off like, and I thought now he'd be worse than ever," Betsy said. "But he didn't act like that at all. In fact, he seemed quite decent for a change."

Pudge didn't say a word. He was thinking about prizes. At first, this one had seemed so important, but now, he knew that it didn't really matter so much. Nick needed to win, of course. There were so many things he didn't have at home— things Mr. Satterlie's money couldn't buy. But Pudge wasn't like that. He had so many things already—things like Dad's and Mom's kind way, the fun they had together as a family, the warmth and love that filled their big kitchen. Those things were more important than any prize in the whole world.

Chapter 12

Christmas with the Buttonwoods

Flora Buttonwood slid behind the table and flopped open the
Sears Roebuck catalog. She was thinking, "Isn't it lucky our
kitchen is so big? If it weren't, we couldn't all get in!"

Even the big Buttonwood kitchen was crowded that evening. Dad Buttonwood sat on the end of the wood box,
whistling half under his breath while he mended Prince's
harness. Mom Buttonwood rocked back and forth, back and
forth. She was darning stockings again. Sometimes it seemed
to Flora as if her mother was always doing that!

The six Buttonwood children spilled all over the rest of the
kitchen. Crish and Peter were sprawled out on the floor,
playing one of their endless games of Uncle Wiggley. Susie

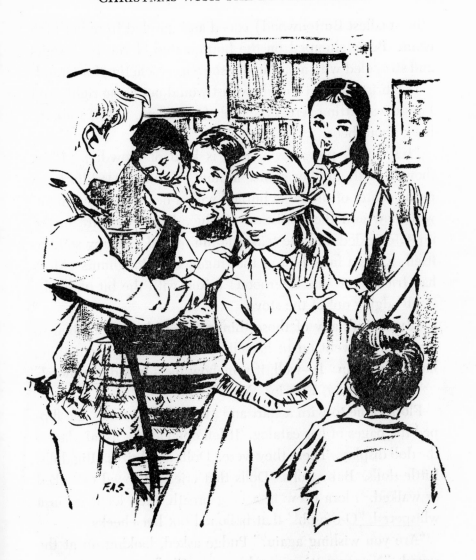

(the smallest Buttonwood) cooed and gurgled from her high chair. Betsy slumped on the bottom step of the back stairs and struggled with a pot holder she was crocheting for Grandma's Christmas that somehow just would not come right. And Pudge was sitting across the table from Flora, lost in a library book about bees.

"It's a nice place, even if it is kind of crowded," Flora thought with another glance around. The big Aladdin lamp in the center of the table burned with a beautiful white light, with now and then a flicker of blue. The wood fire in the range crackled and the teakettle murmured a sleepy song to itself, while a faint hint of the fragance of doughnuts (Mom had fried some that afternoon) mixed with the bit of smoke smell edging out of the stove.

"But it isn't any of those things that make our kitchen so nice," Flora went on to herself. "It's something—something hard to explain. It—well, it somehow feels friendly in here!"

"Daydreaming, Flossie?" Mom asked.

Flora came to with a start and grinned at Mom as she flipped the pages of her catalog. It fell open at the usual place— the doll display. There they were. Dolls of all sizes. Big dolls. Little dolls. Baby dolls. Dolls that cried or cooed or talked or walked. Flora drew in a long breath, then let it go in a whispered, "O-o-o-oh!" that balloned out her cheeks.

"Are you wishing again?" Pudge asked, looking up at the sound. "No use getting your hopes up, Flo."

"I'm just deciding which one I'd choose if I had a magic wish. They're all such darlings." She looked with distaste at her own tattered Priscilla Anne sitting on the radiator. Why, her paint was peeling disgracefully and her clothes were faded and in shreds.

Betsy came over to stand beside Flora. "How about this curlylocks with the blue organdy dress? Or this one. Isn't her green plaid outfit super?"

"Not for me," Flora said firmly. "No bride dolls or boy dolls or character dolls either, thank you. This one's my pick."

She pointed to a blue-eyed bit of a baby doll, perched in one corner of the page. This baby with outstretched arms begged to be held. Her dress was long and dainty, with blue ribbon rosettes fastened in its folds here and there.

"She is sweet," Betsy agreed. "Still, I'm not sure—"

"Honest! To hear you girls, you'd think they were alive." Pudge sounded disgusted.

"Well, there's no harm in wishing." Mom said. "But, Flora, I hope you aren't counting on a doll this year. I don't think we can manage it."

"This one costs only $4.98," Flora said.

"I know. But if we bought you that, we'd want to get Betsy and Crish each one, too. And sleds for the boys—"

"Oh, boy!" Peter looked up. He'd heard only the last words. "Are we going to get new sleds for Christmas, Mom?"

"You are not," Dad said. He stood up and stretched himself. "You'll be lucky if you get an orange and a candy cane each." But his eyes twinkled, and the young Buttonwoods knew that he was joking.

Flora was sure she'd get something more than that. But she also knew she couldn't get the baby doll she really wanted. It seemed as if everything cost so much. Shoes. Groceries. Sweaters. Things you just had to have—so there never was any money left over for the things you really wanted.

Now take Cousin Louise, for instance. She got a new doll every single Christmas, but then Uncle Will had lots more money than Dad.

"Bedtime for everybody under twenty!" Dad said suddenly. "Game's over, Crish and Peter. Hand me the Bible, Flossie."

Flora reached up and took the tattered Bible from the clock shelf above her head. It was old. Dad's grandfather had used it long ago. She had to hold it carefully, so that parts of it wouldn't spill out. There was a newer one in the living room, but Dad liked this one better. Flora could tell by the special look that always came to his face when he picked it up to read.

Crish crammed the Uncle Wiggley board into the toy chest (under the first step of the back stairs) and joined Peter on the wood box. Dad pulled a chair over to the table and opened the Bible, but he waited to begin reading till the giggles and shuffles stopped.

"I am the good shepherd," Dad read. "The good shepherd giveth his life for the sheep—"

Flora leaned back against the wall. The top of the wainscoting made a ridge across the back of her neck, but she hardly noticed. She forgot all about dolls and everything else as Dad read the story about the good shepherd—the same story Dad's granddad had read to his children. Perhaps in a nice big kitchen with a friendly feeling like theirs.

"All of you hop to bed right now," Mom said as soon as family worship was over. She took Small Susie's bottle out of the refrigerator and popped it into the teakettle to heat "Bring me her nightie from the bedroom dresser, Flo. The rest of you scamper upstairs."

Carefully, Flora took a little lamp with a handle from the lamp shelf. She lifted one side of the chimney and pushed a lighted match in. The wick caught at once. It burned with a yellow flame that smelled faintly of kerosene, so different from the white glow of the big Aladdin lamp.

Even with the lamp in her hand, the bedroom was full of shadows. It took Flora several minutes to find Small Sue's nightie and when she returned to the kitchen Mom was alone. She could hear Dad down in the cellar, firing the furnace.

"Mom—" Flora began, then stopped.

"What is it, Flossie?" Mom asked. The big kitchen was quiet—so strangely quiet without the others there.

"Well, I was just wondering about that doll."

Mom's face looked sober. The smile in her eyes went out. "I'm sorry. We simply can't this year, Flo."

"Louise gets one every Christmas." Flora was thinking out loud. "Big beautiful ones. With hair. And lovely clothes."

"Yes, I know." Mom said. "Uncle Will can afford to do that and we can't."

"I wish we weren't so poor." Flora hadn't really meant to say that, but it slipped out before she could stop herself.

Mom was very quiet for a minute. When she did talk, she didn't sound shocked or angry at all. "I know how you feel. I get tired of being poor sometimes, too. But just remember that there are lots of things money can't buy. And we have so much to be thankful for."

The big clock tick-tocked away on its shelf. Mom pulled Small Sue's dress over her head and slipped on her nightie.

"Being together, here in the kitchen on an evening like this is worth a lot," she said.

Then she dropped a quick kiss on top of Flora's head and shooed her off to bed. Flora lay awake a long time, thinking about Louise's dolls and about what Mom had said.

Just as she was falling asleep, she seemed to hear sounds from downstairs. Was that the sewing machine—but why would Mom be sewing at that time of night? Then, the next thing she knew, Dad was calling them all for breakfast, and she couldn't be sure whether she'd really heard anybody or whether she dreamed the whole thing.

The next few days zipped by. When school was over and the holidays began, Mom didn't hurry them to bed quite so fast. The Buttonwoods had high times in the big kitchen of an evening, popping corn and playing games. They spent lots of time making Christmas presents, too.

Then, suddenly, it was the morning of Christmas Day. The minute the little Buttonwoods heard Dad firing the furnace, they were downstairs right away. At first, Mom tried to shoo them back until the kitchen warmed up a little, but at the look on their faces, she gave in.

"Bring your presents over here to the stove," she said.

"I can't imagine what this would be," Flora said. "It feels like an apron or a blouse maybe."

Then she pulled the package open and "Oh, Mom!" was all she could say. Inside was a set of doll clothes for Priscilla Anne, each one as dainty and neat as it could be. There was a jumper and blouse outfit. A pink gingham dress exactly like Flora's latest school dress. A cunning little pinafore and sun bonnet. Two flannel nightgowns. And a warm cape and hood of dark blue wool lined in red.

"Oh, Mom!" Flora said again. "You must have sat up nights, after we went to bed—why, of course. That's what I heard that time when I was wishing for a new doll!"

She hardly had time to look at them all before Mom said, "Now listen. It's a big day—and there are lots of other days when you can play with your presents. So let's bustle around and get our work done before anybody else shows up."

Then, how they all flew around! Before long, a wonderful

smell of chicken and dressing filled the big kitchen. And in no time at all, it seemed, relatives began to show up. Everybody seemed to talk at once—what a noise that made! Mom finally shooed the children into the dining room to play.

"I brought my Christmas doll," Cousin Louise announced importantly.

She showed Flora her newest doll, with yellow curls and a pink silk dress. Flora held her close for a minute.

"Did you get a doll this year?" Louise persisted.

"No-oo," Flora admitted. "But I got some new clothes for Priscilla Anne."

"Really? Let's see them. Cassandra doesn't have a stitch of clothes except the ones she has on—not even a coat. Mother said she just doesn't have time to make any for her right now, either."

Flora hesitated. Priscilla Anne was shabby and old, but she didn't want anybody making fun of her, just the same.

"Well, are you going to show them to me, or aren't you?" Cousin Louise demanded; so Flora had to go.

When she came back, Louise hardly looked at Priscilla Anne. Instead, she grabbed the new clothes and looked them over.

"I wish Mother would make some like these for Cassandra," she said.

"But your dolls always come with such lovely clothes," Flora said. "Cassandra's dress of silk is just splendid, too."

"The doll clothes you buy are always like *doll* clothes," Louise explained. "Haven't you ever noticed? These your mother made are like real clothes. Why, the nighties are just like your own, aren't they?"

Flora still didn't quite understand. She didn't get a new doll often enough to really know what Louise was talking about.

"I tell you what," Louise went on. "I'll trade Cassandra for Priscilla Anne, if you'll give me her clothes, too."

For one minute, Flora felt as if she would just stop breathing. "You wouldn't want to, would you?" she asked.

Louise picked up Priscilla Anne and cuddled her in her arms. She was wearing her warm little cape and hood and in spite of her chipped face, she did look sweet in it.

"Of course, I'd trade," Louise said. "But I know you don't want to."

Flora took a deep breath. As she thought of all the love that Mom had stitched into the little clothes, she put Cassandra down and picked up Priscilla Anne.

"No, I don't," she said. "But you can play with her while you're here."

Poor Louise! Flora felt a little sorry for her because she didn't have Mom to sew for her dolls.

That evening, with the company all gone and the other Buttonwoods busy elsewhere, Flora told Mom about it.

"But why didn't you trade, if you wanted to, Flo?" Mom

asked. "I'm sure Aunt Elizabeth would have allowed you to do it."

"I didn't want to, Mom," Flora said. And suddenly, to her own surprise, she knew that she really didn't. Why, she wouldn't exchange Priscilla Anne for the biggest and best doll in the whole Sears Roebuck Catalog!